SHADOWS ON THE PLAIN

Books by John D. Nesbitt

For the Norden Boys
Lonesome Range
Black Hat Butte
Red Wind Crossing
Rancho Alegre
Raven Springs
Coyote Trail
Black Diamond Rendezvous
Man from Wolf River
Not a Rustler
West of Rock River
North of Cheyenne
Poacher's Moon
Adventures of the Ramrod Rider
A Good Man to Have in Camp
Keep the Wind in Your Face
Shadows on the Plain
Field Work
Blue Horse Mesa: Western Stories
Antelope Sky: Stories of the Modern West
Seasons in the Fields: Stories of a Golden West

Two Novellas:
"Dead for the Last Time"
"Trouble in the Labor Camp"

SHADOWS ON THE PLAIN

John D. Nesbitt

SPEAKING VOLUMES, LLC
NAPLES, FLORIDA
2016

SHADOWS ON THE PLAIN

ISBN 978-1-62815-477-1

for Robert and Jean Gandesbery

Acknowledgments

This collection was originally published by Endeavor Books of Casper, Wyoming, in 2005. Individual stories were originally published as follows:

"Cowboy Heart" appeared in *Deep West: A Literary Tour of Wyoming* (Wyoming Center for the Book/Pronghorn Press, 2003).

"County Plates" appeared in *Emerging Voices*, Spring 2003.

"Light from the Cave" appeared in *Emerging Voices*, Spring 1999.

"Night Driver" appeared in *High Plains Register*, 2004.

"Hunting Along the Wall" appeared in *ReadTheWest.com*, November 1999.

"Chokecherries Are Free" appeared in *Read West Online Magazine*, October 2000.

"Memoirs of the Old Scout" appeared in *ReadTheWest.com*, June 2000.

“One Cold Night at the Quadrille” appeared in *Read West Online Magazine*, December 2001.

Segments of “On the Outskirts” appeared in *Kumquat Meringue*, 1991, and *High Plains Register*, 2005.

“Dusk on the Rangeland” appeared in *ReadTheWest.com*, February 2001.

Special thanks to Bill and Angie Babcock for access to their ranch and its enduring beauty.

Table of Contents

Cowboy Heart 1
County Plates 14
Light from the Cave 28
Night Driver 43
Ice on the Doorstep 57
Hunting Along the Wall 77
Nice Boots 91
Chokecherries Are Free 97
Memoirs of the Old Scout 118
One Cold Night at the Quadrille 138
On the Outskirts 165
Campers 173
Dead Man's Gun 185
Drunk on Christmas Day 202
Dusk on the Rangeland 223

Cowboy Heart

The long shadows of morning lay on the snow as Ryan led the two horses from the stable to the cabin. It was a cold, crisp morning, and the boy could feel the energy of the horses as he saw their breaths rise in clouds. Glancing at the cabin, he saw Vance standing in the doorway. The older man stood with his right arm elevated as he smoked on the stub of a cigarette. The interior of the cabin was dark, so Ryan imagined Vance had turned off the lamp and was pausing with the warmth at his back as he finished his smoke.

As Ryan came to a stop with the horses, Vance tossed the butt of his cigarette into the snow on his right, then stepped forward to take one of the halter ropes. He moved with the smooth, automatic motion of an old ranch hand as he tied the horse to the hitching rail, patted its neck, ran his hand down the horse's shoulder, and took a brush out of his chore coat pocket and started brushing.

Ryan tied off his horse, went to the open doorway, and reached inside to find his brush. The warm air carried the mixed smell of bacon, coffee, tobacco smoke, horse blanket, and saddle leather. The stable was no more than a lean-to, so the ranch hands kept all the tack inside the cabin. Vance said it was just as well that way, as it kept the raccoons from chewing on the salty leather, and a fellow didn't have to shove a freezing cold bit into a horse's mouth.

Ryan liked the whole set-up. He enjoyed the idea of spending most of his Christmas vacation this way—sleeping in a bunk next to a wood stove, whiling away the evening in lantern light, living in the midst of saddles and bridles and ropes and spurs. He liked being away from cars and television. His friends would be going to the mall in Cheyenne or playing basketball in the gym, and he hoped they would think he was lucky to make some money at the same time he was off on an adventure. At least Ryan thought it was a good plan.

Vance apparently thought so, too, in his own terms. The night before, as he had laid his cigarette in the ashtray next to his tumbler of whiskey, he had said, "This is a good way to be, I'll tell ya. Up and away from it all, far from the tents of the wicked."

Ryan was amused by the older man's version of worldly wisdom. Even frying the bacon for breakfast had the quality of a good joke waiting to happen, with a punch line about as funny as being thrown from a horse and breaking a leg. Vance had told a story about working on a ranch where the bunkhouse cook had salted the food too much.

"Everyone was mad all the time, and no one knew why. Then the cook blew up and quit, so we took turns cookin' for about a month, and after a while everyone got back to normal. Then we figured out it was all that extra salt that had us wound up so tight." He lifted all six slices of bacon out of the skillet and laid them on Ryan's plate. "I don't even eat this stuff anymore. The doctors told me to lay off the salt and fat both." Creases came to the corners of his eyes, and the ends of his grey mustache went up. "Course, they tell you to lay off a lot of things. Mainly the things you like the best and can get your hands on real easy."

Ryan brushed his horse and appreciated the warm animal smell on the cold air. He glanced across the horse's back and saw that Vance was gone; then he saw the older man coming out of the cabin and carrying his saddle, blanket, and pad. Vance smiled as if there was another good joke on the way.

Ryan was just getting his saddle in place on the horse's back when Vance came out with the two bridles. Ryan took his and looped it on the saddle horn, then cinched his rig. As he put the bit into his horse's mouth he saw Vance lead his horse away from the hitching rail. Ryan watched the man check the cinch, turn out the stirrup, raise his boot up into place, and pull himself aboard.

"I'll tell ya, kid. You wanta ride every day, 'cause even when you do, the stirrups just seem to get higher and higher."

Their ride took them west through hilly country, where the black cattle were easy to spot against the white snow and pale grass. Nearly all of the cattle were grazing on southern exposures, where the sun was warmer and more of the snow had melted. Vance said the cows were in good shape; he said that was what they were working on right now. The cows had had their calves weaned and had been bred, and now they were putting on a good feed. As long as the weather held out, there wasn't much to do but ride around and take a look.

"Work's too easy right now," Vance said. "You get your guard down. Next thing you know, a big storm can come up, and you wanta have an idea where all these gals are hangin' out." He glanced sideways. "Come a good storm, you'll earn your pay and then some."

Ryan nodded. Come a good storm, and he might wish he had stayed down in the valley. But right now he liked it.

At mid-morning they jumped a mule deer buck, a four-pointer that looked almost as big as a horse as it bounded across the sidehill above the trail. Vance reined his horse, and Ryan did the same.

The old rider motioned with his hat brim and said, "He's a good 'un. He made it through the season."

Ryan watched as the husky deer came to a stop and looked around. "Did you hunt?"

Vance laughed. "When you're this far from town you don't really hunt. You just go out and get camp meat when you need it."

"Oh."

"A nice deer like that one, you like to leave him be. Let him live a little longer and improve the species."

"Uh-huh." Ryan focused on the spot behind the deer's right front shoulder, the spot where he would put the cross-hairs if the moment came to him. Then he looked at Vance.

The old cowboy sat with both hands on the saddle horn. "Those deer have a lot of heart."

"Uh-huh."

The buck went into a trot again, and Vance put his horse into motion. Ryan let his horse fall in as before, and the two ranch hands, one young and one old, continued their ride across the calm, cold country.

They made it back to the cabin at noontime, with a plan to change horses after lunch. Vance heated up a stew of dark meat, carrots, and potatoes. Ryan tasted it and shook some salt onto it. He imagined the meat was venison, and he recalled the big deer they had seen.

"I'd bet if we get a deep snow, those deer'll feel it too." He looked at Vance. "Won't they?"

"You bet they will. They've got more freedom to migrate than a cow does, but they can get stuck."

"I bet."

Vance paused as he cut a chunk of meat in two. "I heard a story one time about a guy who roped a deer off a snowmobile."

"Really?"

"Yeah. This was probably about the time you were born, or a little later."

"Uh-huh."

"The way I heard the story, he rode up to the deer in deep snow, and roped it plumb easy. Then he tied it to his machine and started draggin' it."

"Really?"

"Yeah. Nice guy. He wanted to feed it to his coyote dogs, and he thought he'd have it strangled by the time he got back."

"Wow."

"But when he got there, the deer still had some fight left in him, and he stood up on all four."

"So what did the guy do? Did he shoot it?"

"Nah. He just let a few of his coyote-huntin' dogs loose, and they tore it up." Vance looked straight at Ryan. "A real sport, you know."

"I guess." Ryan imagined the deer making its last stand, choking on a tight rope as it fought off the dogs. He recalled Vance's earlier remark that deer had a lot of heart. "Who'd you hear that story from?"

Vance pushed his plate away. "From the guy's wife."

"Really?"

"Yeah. I was interested in her, and for a while there I thought she might leave him."

Ryan waited and then spoke. "Not a good idea?"

"Damn poor one. Wasted a couple years of my life, just hangin' on the ropes and waitin'." Vance got up from the table and came back with the coffee pot in his right hand. "Damn poor idea. Just tears your guts up, is all. If you think ridin' a horse is hard on your ass, try a no-win love affair." He poured two cups of coffee and sat down. "Or better yet, don't."

"I 'magine. Is she still with him?"

"Last I heard, or wanted to hear." The older man reached his right arm across his chest and held the upper part of his left arm.

Ryan saw the wince of pain. "Are you all right?"

"Oh, yeah. This sonofabitch just hurts once in a while. That's all." Vance moved his hand to the left shirt pocket, raised the flap, and drew out the red-and-white pack of cigarettes. He was smiling again, as if there were a good punch line coming up.

Ryan waited, but the older man said nothing as he shook out a cigarette and lit it. Ryan went back to eating.

Vance set his cigarette in the ashtray and took a drink of coffee. "You know what I think?"

"What?"

"I think we ought to get you in a little ropin' practice when there's not a hell of a lot else to do."

Ryan perked up. "That would be fine."

Vance nodded. "Just practice on a few loose head. No harm in that."

When lunch was done, the older man said he wanted to lie down for a while, so Ryan hauled in firewood and washed the dishes. It was nearly two in the afternoon by the wind-up alarm clock when Ryan sat down at the table to wait.

Vance raised his head and glanced over, then got up from the bunk. As he came to the table, Ryan thought he looked tired. The skin was pale below his brown eyes.

"Well, I guess we'd better get going," Vance said. "I'll go with you to get the horses. I want to get up and move around."

They went to the corral together and caught their afternoon mounts, a bay and a sorrel. Vance was sure-handed as always, but after he tied the sorrel to the hitching rail he went and sat in the doorway of the cabin.

After a few minutes, Ryan asked, "Are you all right?"

"Oh, yeah. I've just got a stomach ache." The old man pushed himself up and went back to his horse.

Ryan thought Vance was still moving around all right as they saddled their horses, but then he noticed the man had stopped and was just leaning with his forearms against the saddled animal. Ryan went around his horse and stood at Vance's left.

The old ranch hand turned toward the boy, and his face looked grey and drawn. "Jerry's not comin' back till the day before Christmas, is he?"

Ryan felt a pang of worry as he shook his head. He had an image of Jerry's pickup, the big white Dodge with four-wheel drive and extended cab. Even in dry weather a two-wheel-drive outfit was lucky to make it to the cabin, so Ryan had left his pickup at the ranch. Jerry had driven him up to camp the day before, along with a supply of grub, and he said he would be back to bring both the hired hands down for Christmas. In the evening Ryan learned that Vance's pickup was at the shop in town getting the clutch replaced. He thought it was real cowboy stuff to be stranded out here with just horses to get around on; now it didn't look like so much fun.

"Do you think we should ride down to the ranch?"

Vance shook his head. "I don't know if I could make it. I feel like a poisoned pup."

Ryan looked at the older man but did not see anything he could understand. "I mean, I'll be right there with you."

"Kid, if I fall out of that saddle, you'll never get me up. And that's how I feel. Weak."

Ryan bit his lip and nodded. "Do you want me to put the horses away, then?"

Vance held the brown eyes steady on him. "No. I want you to ride down to the ranch yourself, and get Jerry to come up here."

Ryan felt his eyes widen. "You mean, just leave you here?"

"That's what I mean." The corner of Vance's mouth jerked back.

"I can't do that."

"The hell you can't. And the sooner the better."

Ryan looked at his horse and back at the old man. "Well, what if something happens while I'm gone?"

Vance took a quick breath through his nose. "You mean, what if I die? Don't be a fool. Everyone's got to die sooner or later anyway."

"But you'd be all by yourself."

Vance turned his head down and to the right as he winced. Then he looked up and said, "Everyone's got to die alone. Even those twins that died in the car wreck a couple years back, each of them had to die on his own. Now get the hell gone."

"Isn't there—"

"Don't make me mad, kid. Why do you think Jerry brought you up here, anyway? He thinks I need someone to keep me company and look out for me. I guess maybe he's right on the second part. Now you get the hell down to the valley and not waste any more time."

Ryan felt the sting of realization. Jerry had hired him to keep an eye on the old man, with any cowboy adventures being secondary. Now the moment had come for him to earn his wages, and he could see there wasn't any point in arguing about whether he should go or stay. "Do you want me to put your horse away, then?"

"No, I can do that. You just git."

By the time Ryan had a bridle on the bay and had swung aboard, Vance was carrying his saddle into the cabin.

All the way down the foothills, Ryan felt the fear of something going wrong and his not being able to help it. He made himself think of his mother and father and sister, and his friends who lived in town, and the girls he knew, but always he came back to the same strong sense of dread. He could picture the old man lying on his back, hands folded, in the darkening room.

He knew he wasn't supposed to run a horse downhill, especially in snow and ice, but wherever it looked like a clear stretch he let the horse out. When he got down to the flat he turned back and looked at the ridge of hills to the west. The sun was going down in a sky of crimson and gold, and the hillsides lay dark in their own shadows. He turned the horse towards the ranch and kicked it into a lope.

* * * * *

The pickup cab was warm and comfortable, with colored lights on the instrument panel and warm air coming out of the dashboard. Ryan could feel himself relaxing from the long ride on horseback, but he felt anxious for the old man. Although the digital clock on the dashboard read 5:48, it seemed much later.

The headlights swept across the snow and sagebrush as Jerry braked and accelerated at every turn. Ryan looked out the side window and up at the sky. The night was dark and clear, and the window glass was cold as he touched it.

"I hope the old man's all right," he said.

Jerry answered without taking his eyes from the road. "He's not that old. He's only fifty or so."

Ryan looked at Jerry. He saw the dark mustache and full cheeks, the husky shoulders and barrel chest. He figured Jerry was somewhere between thirty-five and forty—all grown up and still in his best health. He was like the deer Ryan had seen that morning, full of strength and power.

If Vance was only fifty or so, he wasn't much older than Ryan's father. Still, he seemed like an old man.

Finally the pickup pulled into the camp, and the headlights swept the stable and cabin. Vance had put the horse away all right, but the cabin was dark.

Jerry parked in front of the hitching rail and reached for the flashlight that lay beside him on the pickup seat. He shut off the lights and engine and said, "You can wait here for a few minutes if you want."

Ryan sat in the warm cab, looking out at the night. He had no doubts now that the old man had died, and he imagined the man's spirit floating up into the clear, cold sky. A bright star was shining in the southwest, and Ryan could imagine Vance's spirit making a passage to that star. It would be a cold, lonely flight, but Ryan took comfort in knowing that the old man had not been afraid to die alone.

He imagined Vance had gone in to lie down on his bunk and wait. He wondered if the old man had been mad at him, and then he realized Vance must have sent him away so he wouldn't have to see someone die. If Ryan had waited through to the end, he would have had to ride to the ranch anyway, but in a worse state of mind. Vance had made it easy on him.

The realization made Ryan feel like a kid twice over. He had been sent up to the camp to keep an eye on the old man, and then he had been sent away so he wouldn't have to see the worst of it. Vance had made it easy on the kid, even if it meant dying alone.

Ryan felt a wave of emotion as he thought of the old man, game to the end. It didn't matter that he himself was a kid; what mattered was how a man faced up to things. The old cowboy had a lot of heart. That would be the thing to remember. Even as he thought it, Ryan realized that this moment would stay with him, this moment in which the older man's actions gave their meaning to him.

The cabin door opened, and Jerry's flashlight sent a beam outside. Jerry walked to the driver's side and opened the door. The lights in the cab came on, lighting up the red interior.

"I could use a hand if you think you're up to it."

"Okay." Ryan opened the door and stepped out into the cold night.

Jerry waited at the cabin door with his flashlight beam pointed at the ground. Ryan could see the shadow of the door jamb on the somber grey wood of the closed door.

"This might be kind of hard," Jerry said.

"I can do it," Ryan answered. He thought to himself, Vance did the hard part. He had been brave for someone else's sake. That could be an encouragement for Ryan to do his part now.

County Plates

I had just parked the pickup, gotten Pal unloaded from the trailer, and started brushing him down when the girl, or I guess I should say woman, came over. She was barefoot in shorts and a sleeveless top. She had a full head of brown hair, the color of coffee grounds, and as she got closer I saw she had lively green eyes. And a nice smile.

"That's a pretty horse," she said.

"Thanks. He's a good boy."

"Are you going to take him for a ride?"

"Not exactly. I'm going to load my camp stuff on him, and we're going to pack into the wilderness area a ways."

"That sounds like fun. Just by yourself?"

"The two of us. Him and me."

"Uh-huh. Where do you go?"

"Oh, we follow this trail for about three miles, over the first two mountains. Then we hit the creek and turn right, upstream, and go another mile or so. When we come to a spot that looks isolated and quiet, we make camp."

"Do you mind if I pet him?"

"No, go ahead."

"What's his name?" She was giving him light pats on the neck.

"Pal."

"How old is he?"

"He's nine."

"Is that young or old for a horse?"

"He's in his prime."

She was touching the tip of his velvet nose, tentative-like, with her left hand as she laid her right hand on his neck. "Will he bite?"

"Just apples."

She showed the tip of her tongue for a second and then asked, "What do you do when you're camped all by yourself like that?"

"Not much. As little as possible."

Actually, I make deliberate work for myself, to keep things simple, which is sort of a contradiction, I realize. I like to spend time staring at trees and rocks and listening to the water, sorting things out and letting the unimportant things fall away, but it takes work to be able to do that. I wasn't sure I could make sense of that to her, so I didn't say any more.

I finished brushing and then started combing out his tail. The woman leaned over to touch the callous on the inside of his front leg, and she turned, leaning, to ask me, "What's this?"

"It's something they're born with. There's one on each leg." As I answered I saw that the neck of her shirt had fallen forward to expose her smooth, bare breasts. It was a nice sight, deliberate or accidental.

"Then he hasn't been hurt."

"Oh, no. It's normal."

"My name's Renée," she said, straightened up again.

"My name's Ty, and you already know Pal." I moved forward to brush the mane, and she moved backward to lay her left hand on the lead rope and her right hand on the ridge of his nose. We were only two feet apart, she and I, and there was a current in the air. "Are you camped here in the campground?" I asked.

"Uh-huh. We're in that blue tent over there." She motioned with her hand toward a cheap little A-frame tent at the first camp site. There was a bronze-colored Toyota with Cheyenne plates parked at the site, and as we looked in that direction, a man got out of the driver's seat and came around the car headed toward us.

"Your fellow camper?"

"Uh-huh. That's my boyfriend."

"Oh."

As the fellow came nearer I took a look at him. He was of medium height, maybe five ten, with a slight build. His jeans and t-shirt had a loose fit, and his tennis shoes were untied. His hair, light brown, was thinning. I would guess his age at about thirty—maybe five years older than her. Even as he got closer it was hard to see his eyes, because he wore smoky-tinted glasses, the kind that get darker as the light gets brighter. He was also carrying a beer, a bottle of Miller, in a foam-rubber insulator.

"Checkin' out the new neighbors?" he asked.

"I've always liked horses," she said, rubbing the back of her hand on Pal's soft nose. She spoke across the horse.

I finished combing the mane and walked around the back of the horse to get into the tack compartment of the trailer. "Hi," I said to him.

"Hi."

"Brian," she said, "this is Ty. Ty, this is my boyfriend Brian."

We exchanged glad-to-meet-you as we shook hands, and I tried to get a better look at his eyes. They looked distant, and they did a funny little side-to-side flicker as we made eye contact. But he had a strong handshake.

"The horse's name is Pal," she said.

Brian looked at me. "Would you like a beer?"

I considered the offer. It was a warm day, and this would be my last chance for a beer for a few days. I had whiskey in my camp gear, but a beer was different. I could almost taste the cold drench of it, but I thought better of the notion. "No thanks." I looked up at the sun, as if time mattered, which it didn't. "I've got to be on my way."

"He's going to pack up and hike into the wilderness area," she said to Brian.

"Sounds like fun," he answered, without a great deal of fun in his voice.

"It's all right," I said. Then I leaned over, lifted the front left hoof, and started picking out the caked dirt and manure with the hoof pick. I had my back to Renée, but bent over, I could see her calves and ankles. They looked fine, especially after the boob shot. I almost brushed against her as I ducked under the horse's neck to pick the next hoof. I always start with the front left hoof and go clockwise—it's good to keep all the routines consistent with a horse—so I didn't have to go out of my way to be close to her. Then I was on his side.

"Do you shoe him yourself?" he asked.

"No, I've got a friend who shoes horses."

"Oh. Is it a hard job?"

"Not for him. Or me either, since he does it."

Renée giggled. Brian cleared his throat and spit. I did not feel friendship building. I didn't like him, and I could tell he didn't like me. I wanted to be out of there, away from them—or him, at least.

I cleaned the other two hooves with a few quick strokes, tossed the pick in the tack pail, and pulled out the pad and blanket. I slapped them onto Pal's back and then went back to the compartment for the saddle. On each trip I had to pass between Brian and the horse, and as I pulled the saddle out, he said, "I thought you were going to load him, not ride him."

I got mad too quickly. "How about if I do it the way I want?"

"You can run your finger up your ass for all I care," he said, and he spit and walked away.

I looked across at Renée, who shrugged. Then I walked around the horse's rump to the left side, where I swung the saddle up and let it settle into place. I could see Brian walking away. At about thirty yards he turned and said, "I'll be waiting." Then he moved on.

"I know," she called back. Then she said to me, "He just gets that way."

"If he'd stuck around, he'd see how I pack the horse."

"I'll watch," she said, smiling. "I'll tell him all about it."

I got the saddle cinched down and then brought out the panniers. "These big canvas bags drape over the saddle, and I load the gear into the bags. Then when I get to camp, I still have the saddle in case I want to go on a ride."

"I didn't know you could do things that way."

"It's just one way, but it's the way I do things. Sorry if I offended your boyfriend."

"Oh, don't worry about him."

"I won't."

I had my gear already packed and sorted out, for size and weight, so I wasn't long at getting it all loaded and tied down. Renée hung around and watched, scratching Pal on the jowls and watching me work. Then I locked up the trailer and pickup, got my backpack onto my back, and untied the lead rope.

"Well, I'm off," I said. "Sorry I didn't have time for a beer."

"Somc other time." She smiled, and I saw the tip of her tongue again.

"Sure." I gave a little tug to the lead rope and turned away. Once I looked back to see her nice-looking figure as she walked toward the tent and her boyfriend. What a waste, I thought. Then I made a click-click sound to the horse, and we were off on a hike into the mountains.

It's hard to pinpoint a feeling. I thought I would see her again, but maybe I just had the feeling that I wanted to see her again. At any rate, whether I was expecting to see her or just hoping to, I gave some thought to what I would do if I did see her.

Pal and I camped where we had camped the year before, in the trees on the edge of an open spot, right on Plum Creek. I've never had trouble with him wandering off, so I didn't have to picket him. I just unloaded him, stripped him, and turned him out. Then I set up my dome tent, laid out my bedroll, settled my gear into the tent, and built a small fire in the old circle of rocks.

I cook on a fire, to save on the stove fuel I pack in. A fire is good company when there's no comrade or woman around. And as the night draws in, the fire gives warmth, plus a little smoke to keep the mosquitoes away.

On the first night out I barbecue fresh meat, usually a T-bone. After that it's dry food, like lentils or noodles, jerky, packaged soup, and the like. So I had steak, and a sourdough roll, and an orange—good healthy food in the pure mountain air, with a gurgling stream for music. I made a pot of coffee and set it on the grate. Things had emptied out pretty well so that there wasn't a sense of much more than water, rock, tree, horse, and me. And in a little while there would be stars.

I thought about how she might show up, maybe stepping out of the trees as dusk was thickening. She would be wearing a sweatshirt and windbreaker, blue jeans, and sneakers, with maybe a day pack on her back, too.

She would come on into the camp, take off her pack, and sit facing the fire as she told me how she found her way, based on the description I had given. Things had gotten crowded back at her camp. She thought the guy was crazy, and sometimes he scared the holy hell out of her, especially when he drank. He threw a fit, slamming car doors and breaking beer bottles. He roughed her up a little, not exactly hitting her but grabbing her by the shirt and pushing her up against the car. He didn't like her coming on to another guy like that.

She hadn't known him long, had been living with him for a month. She wanted to get away from him, and now he was drunk and passed out, so she left. I told her I had some extra food, and room in the tent, so she was welcome to stay around until he slept off his fit.

I would fix some more coffee, and she would sit by the fire, hugging her legs and resting her chin on her knees. Then I would let her take the sleeping pad and bag, while I slept on the tent floor next to her in my clothes, using the horse blanket as a cover. I liked the idea of her inside my sleeping bag, with the flannel lining making contact with her bare legs, her bra and panties. Then, of course, after a little while, when I had been a gentleman long enough, she would unzip the sleeping bag and the barrier between us would go away, and we would do the things that a guy thinks about when he's gazing into a fire way out in the mountains.

Then I got to imagining other scenes, in which her boyfriend would come after her. He had a gun, and I didn't know if it was loaded. He started demeaning her, pressuring her to confess what she did with me, threatening to make her do lurid things with him, using words like "I'll make you do what you did that night in the back yard." He would make her holler out that she loved him and that what she did with me didn't mean anything to her. Strange stuff, all of this, but the scenarios made a nice campfire story.

I laughed to myself. I remembered a story I had heard one time, about a friend of a friend. The guy was traveling in Mexico, on the train, and he had a seat next to a woman with a little baby. I don't remember if it was a little boy or a little girl, but it was riding in the mother's lap. The guy thought the woman was nice-looking and probably not very well off, and he thought about how cozy it would be to stop off in a town, put up in a room with her, buy her a nice meal, have a tumble or two in the bed, and pay any extra adjustments on her train ticket. He fell asleep thinking these things, and after a while he felt himself getting bold. Someone was playing with him. He opened his eye just a little bit, I suppose to make some sexy eye contact with the woman, but she was conked out asleep with her head against the window. It was the little baby playing with him. I guess his hot rod cooled down real fast. I remember despising the guy when I first heard the story, what with his condescending ideas of how he was going to patronize this woman and how appreciative she was going to be. My fantasizing about this girl Renée wasn't quite as smug, but I thought I deserved to be laughed at. Women don't show up and make themselves available just because a man would like it to happen—only in fantasies, and common ones at that.

Still, I thought that if I ever saw this girl again, I would want to check it out and see how available she was. I remembered how I had said I was sorry I didn't have time for a beer and how she had said, "Some other time." There had been some kind of a spark there.

* * * * *

I spent four nights at that camp, doing pretty much what I set out to do, which was to listen to the creek and vacate my mind. I washed my face in the cold water from time to time during the day, and I built a fire to gaze at each night, but otherwise I didn't do anything very ambitious.

On the fifth day, I packed up my camp and loaded all the bundles onto the horse. Everything had been just right, I thought—no noise, no interruptions. As I walked back out to the trailhead, I got to thinking about all the obligations I had to go back to—the job, bills, yard work, and such. Like always, I wondered if anything big had happened while I was out of touch. It's rare that I miss anything at all when I'm gone for a few days, but one time I did come back to the news that Princess Diana had died in Paris while I was out staring at a creek and stoking a campfire. On another occasion I came back to a dead battery, which meant I had to sit around for an hour or so until a Forest Service truck came along and I could get a battery jump.

This time, I discovered that someone had vandalized my pickup. At first I thought the sun was glancing funny off my windshield, but then I could see that someone had pummeled it with rocks. It was still in one piece, but it had a network of jagged lines, plus one set of cracks that ran in concentric circles. It looked like a windshield that had been through a bad hail storm, but I knew we hadn't had any violent weather. Looking closer, I saw that whoever had thrown the rocks had also seen fit to trash both my side mirrors. The left one was hanging limp and broken, and the right one was on the ground.

I was sure it was that guy Brian. I flared up just like before, and there I was, at the tail end of a nice camping trip, swearing out loud as I tied up the horse. Calling him a prick. I thought, I didn't make any moves on his little honey. She came over and started the conversation, and even if she did look like a sweet piece of pie, I hadn't been Little Jack Horner.

I remembered Brian and his car both, and I was sure I'd recognize him again. I thought I might even be able to find him in Cheyenne if I went down there some day and looked around. I thought about how a little chicken-necked twirp like that could turn out to be pretty strong, but I knew I could thrash him. When you know you're in the right, you have more confidence. You don't hesitate. You land your punches, or at the very least you slam the little punk up against his car and make him slobber out an apology. That's the way I was thinking.

I was mad clear through, and I guess some of it had to do with the senselessness of it all. Everything had gone just right, with no trouble, and then I came back to this kind of weird revenge. I think some of the strangeness might have come from the isolation. There was no one at the campground for me to even ask a question or two, and there was no explanation except for the damage. I had the whole mess to myself, and I played the same idea over and over, feeding my anger on how I'd like to thrash the guy.

At the same time, I knew I had things to do. I put my backpack in the pickup, unloaded the panniers and saddle, stowed everything, loaded Pal into the trailer, and started the engine. The pickup ran fine, except that I had to crawl all the way back to Laramie peeping through a maze of cracks, with no side-view mirrors to tell me if someone was riding my tail. On top of that, all I could think about was how I could have pounded that jerk.

In Laramie I called my insurance agent, got clearance to get my pickup fixed, and reported the vandalism to the Albany County sheriff's office. I doubted that I would get satisfaction, though. Everyone noticed license plates, but cars from Cheyenne, with a county number of two, were almost as common out in the recreation areas as the Albany County vehicles with the number five. The chances of a deputy noticing a bronze-colored Toyota with county two plates were unlikely, even if the weasel came back to the scene of the crime. Most probably, he would stay away from the Snowy Range for a while.

So I got my mirrors and windshield fixed, and that evening I drove back to Wheatland, where everyone had Platte County plates and waved to each other.

About a month went by without anything coming of the incident. A couple of times I went shopping in Cheyenne, where it seemed as if half the cars were bronze-colored, but I never saw the fellow or his cute girlfriend either one, and I have to admit I still had an eye out for her. Despite the absurdity of it all, I guess I felt someone owed me something out of the mess.

* * * * *

Then one day I was in Chugwater, which is also Platte County. As I rolled into the gas station off the interstate, I felt my pulse jump, like I'd just seen a big buck and it was deer season.

It was this same guy, Brian, gassing up his Toyota. Just by reflex I saw that his license plate was a county two, but I already knew it was him. He was dressed just about like before, with a loose t-shirt and jeans, no cap on his thinning hair, and his smoky dark glasses.

I could feel myself shaking as I parked at the other island. I got out, with my pickup between him and me, pulled the nozzle out of the pump, flipped the lever, and began fueling, as the little message says. Brian looked around, like people do at a gas station, and I could tell he didn't know me from anyone else up here in Platte County.

I wondered if he had his peach of a girlfriend with him. I thought it would be a good scene to call him down in front of her. I kept an eye on him and his car as I filled my tank, but no one else came out of the convenience store. He went in to pay, and I finished putting gas in my pickup. I was still shaking a little. I knew I could have it out with him if I wanted.

I had just slipped the nozzle back onto the pump and was headed for the store when he stepped outside. As he walked toward his car, I didn't have to change directions to come within ten feet of him. It would have been the easiest thing in the world to catch him off guard, maybe say his name or ask him where Renée was. But I just walked past him, wondering if he really had any fight in him. His arms didn't look very strong, and his scalp looked pink beneath his thinning hair.

I let him go by. When it came right to the moment, I went from wanting to have it out with him to not wanting any contact at all. I had that sort of sick feeling that comes when you smell a snake, and I thought, to hell with it.

From inside the store, I had a clear view out the window as he pulled the car onto the road and headed back across the overpass, where the on-ramp led to Cheyenne. Only then did I realize I could have gotten his license number. I let out a short, heavy breath. I thought, it was just as well if I didn't ever see either of them again. If there was anything to feel good about, it was the knowledge that getting satisfaction was just a fancy idea.

Light from the Cave

Clark let himself be talked into doing some traveling. Lennis told him it would be good for the blues. "Get out and around," he said. "You've been moping for almost a year. If she hasn't decided on you by now, what are the chances? Do something for yourself. Eat some new food, take an honest chance at getting food poisoning. Look at women. Get back into the world. Who knows? You might even start feeling normal again."

During spring break they drove down to Chihuahua in Lennis's BMW. It was a comfortable ride, and Lennis talked plenty. He was an art history prof and had been around quite a bit; he knew Latin and German and was fluent in French and Spanish. He acted as if he had seen it all before, and most of it, he had.

They stopped in Juárez so Clark could have an introduction into Mexico. Clark knew enough Spanish to get along, so he told Lennis he'd like to go through the *mercado* by himself.

The shops, or stands, were all together, one after another in the large two-story building. On the second story he got interested in a pair of sandals. He put them on and took a few steps back and forth.

The shopkeeper was an earnest lady, five or ten years older than Clark, maybe forty-five years old. She had a kind, care-worn face surrounded by dark, wavy hair. Her voice was easy to understand. *"¿Le gustan los huaraches? ¿Le quedan bien?"* Do you like the sandals? Do they fit you well?

"*Sí.*" The sandals fit fine, but he hadn't decided whether he wanted a pair. He sat back down.

"All right, take them with you."

"How much do they cost?"

"Twenty dollars."

"Isn't that a little expensive?"

The lady raised her eyebrows, paused, and then answered. "Very well, sir, for you I will sell them for fifteen."

"Won't you let me have them for ten?" He had decided that if he could get the sandals that cheap, he would buy them.

"Oh, no, sir, that can't be done."

He took his feet out of the sandals. "I don't know."

"Very well, sir. I will sell them for thirteen. My first sale of the day."

"I don't think so."

The lady looked at him. "It's my lowest price. Why don't you buy them from me for thirteen dollars?" She said the words "thirteen dollars" in English.

"I don't think so. I'm sorry." Clark stood up.

"That's all right, sir. Something else? A sarape for your wife?"

"I don't have a wife."

"Well, then, a shawl for your girlfriend?"

"That's what I'm missing, a woman." He surprised himself at being so frank.

The honesty came right back, as he saw the kindness in the woman's eyes and felt her speak to him as one person to another. She was no longer trying to make a sale.

"I hope you find her. May God help you."

"Thank you."

In the city of Chihuahua, Lennis found a store that had western boots on sale. With his usual nonchalance and chatting in good Spanish, he tried on half a dozen pairs. A young woman about twenty, with shoulder-length black hair, dark skin, raspberry-red lipstick, and a dark blue dress, waited on him. Her co-worker, who had longer hair, lighter skin, more make-up, and tight blue jeans, looked on. Clark watched them all. Finally, Lennis settled on a pair of plain blue-gray boots with pointed toes and one-inch heels.

The girl in the dark dress turned to Clark. "Is there anything you're interested in?"

Lennis spoke up, laughing. "He's not much of a cowboy. He's still looking for sandals."

"Oh, yes." The girl smiled at Clark. "We don't have sandals, but you can find them anywhere in the city."

"It is a pretty city," he said.

"Thank you."

As they walked down the street, Lennis said, "That was good for your blood, I can tell that."

"There was a lot there, that's for sure. Those women had a lot of presence."

Lennis usually didn't miss a chance to show himself as a connoisseur. "All women have presence, but you feel it more in a Latin country."

"That's why you dragged me here."

Lennis gave him a sharp glance. "You were dying, man. You've let her string you out for nearly a year. Every night she tucks in her kids and goes to bed with her husband, and you sit and think about true love and destiny. I worry about what it's doing to you. Who would I play racquetball with? Schmidt and Hollinger?" Then he stopped in front of a pastry shop. "Let's go in here and find something to try."

They bought eclairs and found a bench to sit on. They were in the center of town, where the cobbled street, closed off to traffic, made a pedestrian thoroughfare. It was a good place to sit on a sunny spring morning, eating pastry and watching the people of Chihuahua walk by.

After the pastry, Clark licked his fingers while Lennis lit a cigarette.

A woman in her late fifties or early sixties, dressed in black but not drab, stopped in front of them. She had silver-streaked dark hair, fair skin, even teeth, and a soothing, melodious voice. "How it pleases me to see two young men admiring the landscape!" She nodded and smiled at both of them as she spoke.

"*Muchas gracias*," Lennis said.

"*Que les vaya bien*," the señora said as she walked on. I hope all goes well for you.

"*Y a usted*." The same to you. Then Lennis turned to Clark. "I think she meant the women."

"It seemed like it. There are a lot of them to watch." Clark knew that Lennis wanted him to take more interest in the sights he had brought him to see, but Clark couldn't make himself feel the way someone else wanted him to.

* * * * *

Lennis had said all women had presence, but by mid-morning of the second day, Clark began to wonder about one kind of woman. It was the Indian women; he had seen several of them in Juárez, also. They were a separate case, these tough, impassive women who went barefoot in their native dresses, often with a child slung in a bundle or clutched by the hand. It was always a woman with a small child or children—no men, no older children—asking for handouts but no pity. They seemed hard, almost sexless, in contrast to the warm, compassionate Hispanic women.

Clark asked about them. Lennis said, yes, that was the way they came to town. They were an independent, non-conformist, give-a-damn sort, he thought, who looked at begging differently than an Anglo might. It was work, not charity.

In a shop where Clark bought a small onyx burro for his niece, Lennis asked the storekeeper about the Indians. The man was clear-eyed and clean-shaven, dark-skinned, and neatly dressed in a striped short-sleeve shirt and a pair of slacks. He said the Indians were Tarahumara. He went on to explain that they were indeed independent, proud and self-sufficient; that they made their own clothes as well as other crafts; that they sold their wares in town and then went back to their pueblos. He referred to them as *gente indígena*, indigenous people, and nowhere in his answer did he have a trace of condescension.

Then, that afternoon, Clark saw two women who changed his view of the Indians, although he couldn't have said what the view had changed to. The women, dressed in their garb, were resting in the shade in a plaza a few blocks from downtown. Their children were stretched out on the grass, sleeping. One woman was sitting straight up on a curb that ran between the sidewalk and the grass. The other woman was lying on the lawn, leaning on a bundle, looking at her friend. They were smoking cigarettes and talking, almost laughing.

Lennis seemed determined to meet a woman in Spain. He acted as if the excursion to Mexico had been a prelude to the real thing. In a way it was, as he was going to Spain for six months on a sabbatical, to study cathedrals and indulge his interests.

"You'll like Spanish women even better," he assured Clark, as he tried to convince him to go.

Clark was still strung out, to use Lennis's phrase, and the biological interests weren't perking in him as they were in his friend. But he agreed to go along for a while, right after school got out. He didn't have anything definite in mind—certainly nothing as purposeful as Lennis did—but he thought he should be doing something, and he imagined that in some way the experience would be worth it.

As expected, Lennis knew all the ins and outs of double-dipping into research grants and sabbatical money, finding cheap plane fares, leasing a car, renting a *piso*, or flat, and moving through the hubbub of bustling Granada, where he based their visit. Clark was to stay two weeks. After that, Lennis would begin his serious academic study, but in the meanwhile he was taking his leisure and observing the cultural landscape.

As always he was reposed, affecting an air of carelessness. "*Descuidado, sí; descarado*, no," he joked. Careless, yes; impudent, no. He jaywalked, double-parked, tossed live cigarette butts onto the sidewalk—all in the custom of the country. He kept Clark out until four in the morning, drinking and chatting with Germans at an outdoor table below the Alhambra. He had him drinking before noon as well, but never drinking hard. He versed Clark on the words for short beer, tall beer, and bar snacks. He instructed him not to tip much. Just as casually he re-corrected his vocabulary: here it was *pasteles* and not *postres* for pastry, *profesor* rather than *maestro* for the work they did. (In Mexico, Clark had asked how to describe himself, a learning skills director, and Lennis had said, "Just say *maestro*. Save yourself some trouble.")

Clark, who had been at most a casual Presbyterian, always felt like an intruder when it came to sight-seeing in the churches. Lennis, of course, had no qualms. "I don't want to drag you to a lot of these," he said, "but there's a church here that has an androgynous Christ. You'll love it." He paused at a corner. "I'll bet a *caña* there's a gypsy woman sitting by the door. There always is."

They turned the corner and there, sure enough, was a swarthy woman with unkempt hair and baggy clothes, sitting by the door and breast-feeding a baby. Lennis dropped a coin into her cigar box.

Inside the church, they saw life-sized figures of Christ and the virgin.

"This one?" Clark whispered as he indicated the statue.

"No. I meant a painting."

"Oh." They walked on.

At one niche, an older woman knelt at an altar that held several lit candles. As the woman rose and turned to leave, Clark recognized the white hair and blue eyes of the woman who had sold him some dried fruit earlier in the day. He nodded and she nodded back.

People seemed to be gathering in the church for an evening service. Lennis stopped in his stroll, looked around with a half-frown, and said in his low voice, "Damn. I've got my wires crossed. That painting isn't here. I remember where it is now."

"Where?"

He shook his head. "It's too stupid a mistake for me to tell you. But it's not here." He headed for the door.

It was the only time Clark had known him to make that sort of error. "It's no big deal."

"Oh, no. And you still owe me a beer. The gypsy woman was there, just as I said."

After the mistake about the painting, Clark thought Lennis was being more attentive. Then he realized that Lennis had, in his own way, been paying more attention than he had in Mexico, but not in the direction of art and monuments. It seemed to Clark that Lennis had his pheromone sensors turned on and the distraction had caused him a lapse in an area where he was usually infallible.

On one excursion they drove past La Peña de los Enamorados, the legendary rock mountain. Lennis told a short version of the story, about a Christian man and a Moorish woman who fell into forbidden love in Granada, fled the city and came to the Rock of the Enamored, or Lovers' Cliff, and plunged together to their deaths.

On down the highway they stopped in the town of Antequera, where they went into a *café bar* and stood at the counter. An indifferent woman of about forty served them coffee with hot milk.

Lennis said, "They're only that way on the surface, the Spanish are. Once you break the ice, it's an entirely different story."

Clark nodded. He looked at the woman, who was watching the television. She had a light complexion and dark eyes, and her black hair was combed back and tied. She wore a white apron over a pale green dress, and she seemed to have a slender, shapely figure.

Lennis spoke to the woman, asking her to tell the story of the ill-fated lovers.

The woman's features came to life. "Are you two from France?" It was not the first time someone had thought they were Frenchmen.

"No, we are North Americans."

"*Bueno*." The woman took on the air of a person about to tell a story clearly and simply, by widening her eyes, smiling, and dipping her head. "*Hace siglos, en la ciudad de Granada, se enamoraron dos jóvenes. Un cristiano*," she brandished a finger, "*y una mora*." She shook her head. "*Pero el amor fue prohibido. Los enamorados huyeron de Granada, hasta aquel peñasco, y allí se arrojaron, juntos, a la muerte*." She smiled and tipped her head, by way of closure. She had told the story very much as Lennis had.

"A charming story," Lennis said, still in Spanish. "Thank you."

"You're welcome. It is a famous legend."

Back on the road, Lennis lit a cigarette and held it in his left hand on the steering wheel. Then, holding his right hand out with thumb and fingers pursed upwards, he said, "That woman had real presence, to use your word. She really had it."

"Your type?"

"Not entirely. She'd have to be at least ten years younger. But there was some real spirit there."

Clark looked at the road map he had spread out. "I guess."

Later that day, at Ronda, they bought bread and cheese and fresh peaches near the famous bull ring. The girl who sold them the groceries was about eighteen, by Clark's estimation. She had a nice figure, set off by a cotton blouse with the tails knotted above the waist of her jeans. She wore scarlet lipstick and smoked a cigarette. It seemed as if everyone in Spain smoked.

Lennis said to Clark, in reference to the peaches, "Call them *melocotón* in this country."

The girl brightened. "*Sí, melocotón*."

Lennis assumed his explanatory air. "We're from the United States. In the new world they say *durazno*."

The girl smiled and blew out smoke. "*Claro*." Of course.

They ate their lunch on the brink of *la ventana del coño*, the dizzying gorge that the town overlooked. As they ate, Clark asked, "How about the girl who sold us the peaches? Did she have it?"

"Too young." Lennis cut all the way around his peach, opened it into its two halves, thumbed the pit onto the cement at their feet, and said, "And besides, I think the little bitch shortchanged me a hundred pesetas." He bit into the first half and then asked, as he chewed, "How about you?"

"She was all right. But I think you're more tuned into the women here."

"What do you mean?"

"I didn't see much difference between her and the woman at breakfast. If anything, I liked the girl better, but even she didn't do much for me."

Lennis paused with the peach halfway to his mouth. He arched his eyebrows and smiled. "My God, Clark, I drag you all the way to this part of the world to try to educate you on these matters, to breathe some life into your walking corpse, and you fail to grasp the lesson."

"The woman at breakfast had it, and I missed it, huh?"

"Sadly, you brute."

"Maybe I have to be hit over the head with it, like in the boot store in Chihuahua."

Lennis paused and then said, "Oh, yes. Those two. So *that's* where you are in all of this."

Clark smiled, almost laughing. "I guess so."

"Well, that helps us decide where we'll go this afternoon. We'll indulge your interest in things primitive, and we'll go to La Cueva de la Pileta. I've been there only once myself, fifteen years ago, and I'd like to see it again."

* * * * *

The tour guide explained that the cave had been inhabited by humans some twelve thousand years earlier, had vanished from modern memory, and had been rediscovered at the beginning of this century. All efforts were being made to leave the cave as it had been; thus there were no electric lights, and some of the group would be asked to carry lanterns. Lennis took one, as he and Clark fell in at the end of the group.

The cave was known for its etchings, which fascinated Lennis but held very little meaning for Clark. Most of the marks were short black strokes of a hieroglyphic nature, with here and there a stick figure of a person, or a profile of a horse or goat. Some of the animal drawings were pale orange or yellow, and many did not outline the whole animal.

Then came a moment of magic. The guide told them, in his jaunty way, "*Vengan aquí adelante, para a-lum-brar este dibujo.*" Come on ahead here, to light up this drawing.

There, behind an overhang of rock, drawn against a smooth wall, was the full outline of a pregnant horse. The side of the horse was marked up with red and black strokes which may have meant something. But the belly—Clark knew it and understood it all at once. It swelled like a mare's and yet like a woman's. The painting spoke to Clark with no ambiguity; it conveyed the element that linked the artist to the horse to the woman to the cave-dwellers to the people in white tennis shoes.

"That was a pretty funny joke," Lennis said as they moved on.

"Which one?"

"*Alumbrar.* It means to illuminate or shed light. But it also means to give birth. *Dar a luz* means the same thing."

"Oh."

"That was his joke, when he told us to step up and show some light."

"He seems to be fairly witty."

"He has his jokes pretty well worked out."

"Lennis, I can't believe that horse."

Lennis looked at him in the lantern light and then nodded. "It's incredible, isn't it? You connected, didn't you?"

"I sure did."

"I remember the first time it happened to me. I was up in the Basque country, which gives you a prehistoric feeling in its own way anyway. I was on a cave tour, and I saw a hand print that had been drawn over fissures in a rock, cracks that were just like the lines in the palm of your hand. I felt as if I could have laid my hand on that print, and connected with the artist. There's a real feeling there."

"That's the way that horse worked for me."

At the end of the tour, Lennis turned in his lantern and bought a postcard while Clark waited. Then they went outside, where Clark saw the world again in its literal details—a dirt path leading down a rocky hillside to the parking lot. Lennis was his nonchalant self as he bleated to two kid goats that stood on the pathway. He took out a cigarette, broke it in two, and gave a half to each goat.

"Tell me something, Lennis."

"Yeah?"

"You saw that drawing before?"

"Uh-huh."

"Did you remember it?"

"I saw the hand on that same trip, and I remembered it better. You know, from time to time, place to place, you tune in differently."

"I guess so."

* * * * *

For as much as Clark seemed to lack a woman in his life, he failed to grasp the lesson, as Lennis had said the day they bought the peaches. But the image of the horse stayed with Clark through the rest of his visit—as they went to the Mediterranean, to the mountain villages of Las Alpujarras, back to Granada and the Alhambra. Then he left Lennis to his study of cathedrals and his quest to meet the Spanish woman. As Clark was on the flight back to New York, he had time for deliberate thought about the horse. *Alumbrar. Dar a luz.* Illuminate. Give to light. In its own language the drawing was about the gypsy woman with the baby, the girl who sold them the peaches, the girls in the boot store, and all the other women they had seen; but it was also about the guide himself, the cave-dwellers he had described, the man who had sold Clark the onyx burro, the native people he had talked about. It was about Lennis; it was about the artist; and it was about Clark, a woman who would probably never be his, and a woman he was yet to meet.

Night Driver

When I thought of Duck Logan, I often pictured him in the cab of a cattle truck, driving the narrow highways in the lone hours of the night. I knew what the trucks from the 1940's looked like because they were still around when I was growing up. They were always dark—black or deepest green—and not much different in style from a pickup or a one-ton or a bobtail. A truck from that era had a narrow cab, a long nose, bug-eye headlights perched in the slopes between fenders and grille, and a wide chrome bumper. Small, round mirrors stuck out on spindly arms, and a canvas water bag might be slung on the front bumper or on the spotlight mounted on the driver's door next to the hood. A white wig-wag signal arm, shaped like a necktie and studded with three or four reflectors, hung outside the cab and was operated by a cable from within. I pulled on a few of those cables myself.

The trucks I got to know were worn out, with a rattle in the body or engine, but the ones Duck showed me in his pictures were newer, trim and tight. "Damn good one," he would say, the smoke curling up from the cigarette between his fingers as he pointed. "Bought it new and drove it back from Indiana." He was proud of having had good trucks, and I could look at one of them in the picture and think of how it had been a refuge for him as he carried his sorrow around.

When I worked with him he was in middle age, and he seemed to think of his life as being in two parts: the first half, when he had trucks and horses and money, and the second half, when he worked for wages and lived alone. From the anecdotes he told me and the details I picked up elsewhere as I worked on the farms and ranches, I pieced together the main stories of his early life.

I've often thought of myself as a sort of collector of life histories, the kind of person who files things away and accumulates knowledge. I seem to be the type that people like to tell stories to. I imagine it's because I show interest and have a detail to contribute here and there myself. But up until recently I've never been one to pry, and I wouldn't want someone to think I was when I wasn't trying to. I've held it as a point of pride that I let the stories come to me. In the long run it's not a hard way to do things, because most people are willing to tell stories, either about themselves or someone else, and a fellow can put together quite a bit without ever being nosy.

Duck wasn't the type to jabber all day long, like some men, but we spent a lot of time together fixing fence, irrigating, working on equipment, and driving from one field to another. At lunch time or on a smoke break, he would tell some part of one of the larger stories I put together. He always wore long-sleeved shirts of dark, heavy fabric, some of them with the old style of long collars and all of them with two chest pockets with flaps. In the left pocket he carried a pack of Pall Malls, unfiltered, and in the right he carried Salems, which were filtered menthol. Through the day he would go to one pocket or the other, for the red pack or the green one, as if every decision in life had two options and a person could pick one and be sure of it. But I could never predict which pocket he would go to—I suppose it was just a matter of how his lungs felt at the moment—and I never found a correlation between the kind of cigarette he chose and the kind of story he told with it.

Most of his stories were related in one way or another to that period in his life when he had the trucks and drove all over the country buying and selling cattle. I can still hear the rasp in his voice as he began with the words "When I was in the cattle business." He talked about the way things were done back then—the stock racks were all made of lumber, and no one had double- or triple-deckers. People just laughed when he said he wished he could get some built. Some stories had something happen in them, such as the time a big trucking outfit lost three rigs when they piled up on one another at the bottom of a steep grade, but a lot of them were just sketches of a time when a man could buy cattle on a three-day draft and beat it to the bank. Then within that broad group of stories were sets, each of which made up a story in itself.

Of these, the most serious story was one about a girl he was going to marry but didn't get to. This was the first of three great setbacks in his early life. Although I learned some things about Duck from other people, I heard very little of this story from anyone but him. The girl's name was Dottie, as I found out later, but he never referred to her as anything but "the girl who died." He usually lowered his voice for those words. The girl was a couple of years behind him in school, and they were waiting for her to graduate and turn of age, and then they were going to get married. But she got sick with a case of appendicitis, which was a lot more serious back then, and she never made it out of the hospital. He told me how some of the folks from her family went out to the place where he and his father and his brother Mickey were working on a windmill, and they told him she died.

That was the beginning of a deep sorrow that threaded its way through the rest of his life. He told me he never drank before that but he did from then on. He used to buy a fifth of whiskey, drive out to the cemetery at night, and drink the whole bottle by himself as he sat by her grave. When he was sober, driving the narrow highways at night, he would have visions of her in her casket, appearing in front of him in the headlights. I imagined him, tensed in the dark cab, straining and blinking, taking deep breaths and driving on. He said it wracked the hell out of him, and even though he tried to get to know other women after that, he didn't get very far with any of them. "It was never any good," he would say, with a tight set to his mouth and a slow shake of the head. By and by he learned that the one way he could deal with women was to pay them, and that kept things uncomplicated.

At about the time he was trying to get over the girl who died, about two years later, his brother Mickey died in a car wreck. Duck did not talk much about the incident, and when he did he usually referred to it as part of some other story, such as, "My brother was supposed to haul a truckload of dry cows down from Rapid City, but that was the weekend he died." Most of my knowledge about the accident, then, came from other people. The simple version of the story was that Mickey was driving too fast on the River Road, and the more hushed version was that he might have been chasing another car, which, of course, might have had a girl in it, on the passenger side.

The brother's death was a double blow for Duck. Not only did he lose his brother, but he also lost his partner in the cattle business. Their father was old-fashioned and stuck in his ways, and he didn't want to take the risks of buying here, selling there, and always trying to beat the clock. But the brothers were young, and they had guts. Between the two of them they could cover a lot of country, and they were out to "make a shit-pot full of money."

So Duck was on his own then, in the early 1950's. The cattle market wasn't in good shape because Truman was going to set the price on cattle and no one wanted to get stuck. That was how Duck explained it to me, that everyone wanted to sell and no one wanted to buy. He said he knew a guy named Stanley, who was a high-up bookkeeper for a big sale yard in Idaho Falls, and this fellow told him the market was going to drop and then come back up again. The thing to do was to go out and buy up all the cheap young heifers he could find, put 'em out on pasture, and then wait things out. Duck had two trucks, some money, and some nerve, but he didn't have any pasture. Stanley said that was fine, he knew someone who could handle five hundred head in eastern Idaho and western Wyoming. He himself had to stay out of the light because of his job, but he could make the connections and they could split the profits.

So Duck went out and bought cattle. "People must've thought I was crazy, which I would've been if I thought I was going to turn around and sell 'em." When he had nearly five hundred head sitting in the pens at half a dozen different stock yards, he called up Stanley to find out where to haul them. Stanley asked him what he meant, that he never said such a thing, and if Duck had gone out and bought like that when the market was the way it was, he hoped he could get out of it all right.

Duck, who had always operated on the old code of a man's word and a handshake, told me, "I never understood how a man could do that." At first he thought Stanley had found someone else to work with, and then he figured the man had gotten a clearer indication that the market wasn't going to come back up soon enough—which it didn't—and rather than admit he was wrong, he left Duck to take the loss. Which he did. With no place to take the cattle and with prices no better in one place than another, he had to turn around and sell them where they were. He lost anywhere from seven to fifteen cents a pound on every one of them, he said, and it left him "flat-ass broke." He had to sell the trucks to try to pay some of his losses, but he still lost everything including his credit.

All the spiraling down took a while, and I understood that he might have done some drinking as things went to hell, but when he hit the bottom he stayed there. He told me about one night, not long after the first big plunge, when he sat at home with his deer rifle in his lap and thought about "goin' to look up that fella Stanley." He said he was sober that night and thought about it long and hard, and in the end he decided it wasn't worth it. For one thing, he thought he might get back on his feet some day, and for another, he had his pride and was going to take this loss as he had taken others.

By the time I met him, fifteen years later, it was evident that he didn't ever get back up. As I saw it, he had been hit too many times and too hard.

When I knew him, he was gray-haired, wore bifocals, and had wrinkles in his neck. He lived in a little cabin court at the edge of town. It wasn't as shabby as it is now, but it had already turned into the kind of place that rented by the week and by the month. More than once I stopped long enough to drink a six-pack and to see the pictures of the cattle trucks, the pinto and buckskin saddle horses, and the Packard that would "turn a hundred easy." He lived alone with his memories and died that way.

Among those photos I am sure I never saw a picture of the girl who died, and I am pretty sure I never saw one of his brother. Nevertheless, I thought I had Duck Logan's story put together: early prosperity, three hard falls, and then a long stretch of wage labor, used cars, and old clothes. I thought the biggest thing in his life was the girl dying, and after that, the way he went broke. They seemed the biggest because of the way he talked about them, but as I look back I can't be sure.

* * * * *

A few years after Duck Logan died, some thirty years after I first met him, I began to piece together another little history, which at first seemed unrelated to his. The story started to take shape one day when my girlfriend, Joanne, was telling me about a realtor who had just died in her home town. It was the kind of story I listen for, so I followed it with interest.

The realtor's name was Richard Lawrence, and he was in his seventies when he died. I knew him from when he was in middle age and used to sell property over this way. I remembered him as a glad-hander sort, as his kind often is, smiling and giving a pat on the back. He had good teeth, good hair, good clothes, and a good car to drive people around in. Naturally, when a story about someone like him comes around, I'm waiting for the other part.

As Joanne heard it from her mother, Shirley, this fellow Richard was Shirley's boyfriend in high school, and then they went their separate ways. About twenty-five years later, when Richard was in his forties—which would have been about the time I saw him styling around with prospective buyers of property—he went back to Shirley and threw himself at her. His wife had left him, and he had looked into his heart and realized he had never loved anyone as much as he had loved Shirley.

"And what did she say?"

"She just about laughed in his face."

"Oh, really?"

"Sure. All the time they were goin' together—at least the way she told it—he didn't get what he wanted from her, so after he took her home from a date, he'd drive over here to Elkhorn and get it on with a girl he knew in town."

"Wow. I bet he lead-footed it all the way. A rocket in the pocket."

"I guess. There's my mom, going to bed and thinking about her sweetie-pie, and here he is, forty miles away, romping on Patsy."

"Then she found out?"

"Not right away, but when she did, it sure finished things for good."

"I should hope so."

"Well, they're both gone now, and who knows how things went for him after she turned him down that last time."

"Oh, I'm sure he got by."

"Oh, yeah. I doubt that he died of a broken heart."

That little piece of story gave me some satisfaction, as it helped me confirm the impression I had that Richard Lawrence was a phony. Then another detail in the story clicked for me.

"Huh. Did you say the girl's name was Patsy?"

"Yeah. She was one of the Tidwells."

"Oh. Uh-huh." I didn't say anything more, but it set me to thinking. According to the old stories, Patsy Tidwell was the girl who might have been in the car that Mickey Logan might have been chasing. It seemed to make sense. If she liked to take another girl's boyfriend, at least for the amount of time that she was in the back seat with him, maybe she liked to play one guy against another. And maybe Richard Lawrence was driving the car she was in.

It fit all too well. The glad-handing, two-faced son of a bitch. I could imagine him, seeing the other car as it rolled off a narrow curve in the highway, and then driving on just to protect his own ass. For Duck's sake, I felt some contempt for Richard Lawrence.

It held my interest, this possibility of a three-way intrigue between Richard and Patsy and Mickey, but then I caught myself thinking I had arrived at a conclusion. More out of a sense that I should verify my own theories than out of a feeling that I should be fair to Richard, I thought I should do some checking.

I went to the cemetery first, where I found Mickey's headstone and learned that he had died on September 29, 1950. While I was at it, I paid my respects to Duck, now in his grave off by himself, and then it occurred to me to look up the girl who died. Her name, I recalled, was Dottie, which would be Dorothy. She was an Anderson, and when I found their plot I found her. She died on July 13, 1948. Then I went to the newspaper office and, looking in old yellowed copies, learned that Mickey died on a Friday and Dottie died on a Tuesday. I didn't think the day of the week mattered very much, but being in touch with that much detail, through their gravestones and the newspaper articles from the time, gave me the feeling that I knew more about what little I started with.

By now I realized I was going out of my way more than I usually did to put together someone else's story, and I realized I was checking the Patsy story against what I thought I knew from Duck's story. And it all checked out. The girl died in the late 1940's, the brother died a couple of years later, and the crash in the cattle market would still have fallen in the Truman years.

But I wasn't satisfied. I wanted to know whether Richard had been in the car with Patsy; I might even say I was eager to know it. All of these people were dead now, including Patsy, who had moved away long ago but whose obituary made it into the town paper. So I decided to go to a place where all the old-timers hang out in the afternoons. It's a café and bar, with pool tables and a card table. I went there one day when the livestock sale was over, and I took a barstool in the midst of the cigar smoke and chit-chat.

In a little while I singled out a man who looked like he would be old enough. He was wearing a light-colored, short-brimmed hat and a wool shirt with a string tie, and he had a very pale complexion. I thought I knew who he was, but I wasn't sure. He looked like Dale Curwood, who for many years had been on the County Fair Board and had ridden his horse in the parade. I took a stool next to him, found out that he was indeed Mr. Curwood, and introduced myself. He seemed pleased with himself and everything he knew, and after flattering him on his knowledge of town history, I asked him if he remembered Patsy Tidwell.

"Oh, Patsy," he said, with a flicker of the eyebrows. "Sure I do."

I told him I was trying to fill in a few blanks in my own family history and I was wondering if she had ever been involved with any of my family members, whose names I would rather not volunteer in this place at this moment.

He gave a wise nod and rotated his glass of whiskey and water. "Oh, she was quite a little run-around," he said.

"That's what I understand. I guess she always liked to have more than one on the line."

"More than one, I should say. More like three or four, and she wanted to keep each one secret from the other."

"Oh, is that right?"

"Oh, yeah. That was her style. She always liked to have secret boyfriends. Maybe one in this town, one in the next."

"That's kind of what I gathered."

"Uh-huh. There was a time when she was supposed to be engaged to a fellow over in Glennville, and then when either of the Logan brothers was in town, she'd sneak out with them."

"The hell. Did she go out with both of 'em?"

"Oh, yeah. On the sly. And that guy in Glennville was the biggest fool of 'em all. But even he got smart, and she had to find someone from far away who was dumb enough to marry her."

"Women can do it."

"You bet they can."

I bought Mr. Curwood a drink and eased out of the conversation. I felt I had gotten more than I wanted, but I also knew I was hooked on the story and needed to know more. That evening, I brought up the topic with Joanne.

"So when did Richard use to come over here and diddle Patsy?"

"Oh, it was before my mom got married."

"I mean, like the year or years."

"Well, my mom got married in 1949."

"Then that was a few years before you were born."

"Sure. She had Barbara, Judy, Marilyn, then me, then Steve."

"Oh, uh-huh. And when did Richard get married, or do you know?"

"Not long after she did. He found someone else to help him get over her. He's got kids that were in the same grade as Barbara and Judy, so he didn't waste any time."

"Then he probably wasn't coming over here in, say, 1950, and he sure wouldn't have been engaged to Patsy at that time."

"No, not at all. And I doubt that he would ever be engaged to her anyway. Why?"

"Oh, I just heard a story about her today, and I don't think it was any earlier than 1950. She was supposedly engaged to some guy from over there."

"I don't know who that would be, but it wouldn't have been Richard."

"Do you think he would have been coming over here at all, for that purpose?"

"I don't know. He had a pretty full plate by then and would have been staying close to home, but I wouldn't put it past him to try to get in a quickie."

That much helped, to be able to get in another jab at Richard, but it didn't help me place him in the other car. I doubted that he would have been over here on a Friday night, cruising around like a single guy. It would have been more his style to get a nooner.

What bothered me more than my lack of convincing evidence about Richard was an awareness that was setting in. I couldn't prove that Mickey's brother was not in the other car.

I didn't like to have to consider that possibility, but as I had thought before about Richard, it could fit. I had always liked Duck, and whether he was in the other car or not, or whether there even was another car, I felt I had gone farther than I should have. I thought, what business did I have, thinking I could really know someone else's story? I felt as if I knew more about his truck than I did about him, and I wished I could go back. It had been better when I could think of him as a man who drove a dark cattle truck and nothing more, a young man whose girlfriend had died and who nursed himself on the sadness of it as he drove through the long, lonely stretches of the night.

Ice on the Doorstep

Clark told himself he was going to have to kick things in the ass to make any change at all. He had been going around in circles, coming back to the same dead feelings, and he thought a road trip might get him on a straight line somewhere. The way he had it mapped out in his mind, the road from Cheyenne to Albuquerque took a couple of big turns, but overall it made a line south. A right turn in Albuquerque would send him on another straight shot to the west. He had nothing so formal as an interview, just an open invitation to come and look over some facilities in Flagstaff, but it was something. When spring break came around, he put in for a couple of days extra, locked up his house, and got out onto the highway toward Cheyenne.

An hour and a half later, he filled up the tank at the Flying J, then pulled onto the interstate again. As he passed the bison ranch south of Cheyenne, he settled in for the six-hour stretch through Colorado. Unless the coffee got to him sooner, he would stop in Pueblo. He could drive all the way from Cheyenne to Ratón without stopping in Colorado if he wanted. He had done it once. That was a while back, when he was always in a hurry to go from place to place, even on long trips when he did not expect to meet anyone.

He looked in the rear view and saw a car coming up on him. It pulled into the left lane and went around him, a grey Chrysler with Montana plates, and a film of road grime all along the side panels. That guy was moving. Maybe he had a girlfriend in Texas.

Having a girlfriend somewhere wouldn't be so bad. After going through the wringer with Delia, as he had come to call her, sometimes he thought any woman would do. Then after a night on the town, seeing the bars full of people who thought the same way, for many of the same reasons, he would wake up alone in his bed and think it was just as well for the time being. But as the song said, there was probably life out there somewhere.

Now a big truck loomed in the rear view, moved over a lane, and thundered past. Clark saw the blue letters of a Wal-Mart truck. According to the propaganda, Wal-Mart drivers were true knights of the road, caring nothing for their own time as they helped single mothers, senior citizens, German tourists. It was good to know there was so much help at hand. As he crossed into Colorado, Clark saw two more trucks with the same blue letters headed north.

Sunshine came in through the windshield and cheered the atmosphere. The day was not warm, but it was sunny, and the road was dry. As he passed the Budweiser brewery in Wellington, Clark tuned in a radio station from Denver. A song came on that he had not heard before. It was a slow number, set to the tune of a mountain ballad and consisting of a lone singer and his guitar. The fellow was looking out his window at sunset, thinking about ice on the doorstep, frost on the pane, and a woman he was trying to get over.

When the song ended, it was followed by George Jones with "She Thinks I Still Care" and Jim Reeves with "He'll Have to Go." With the sun streaming in and the Motel 6 and Denny's floating by on the first Fort Collins exit, it seemed as if everything was in its right place—maudlin songs and mundane stopovers, all of it a little too real to laugh at.

* * * * *

As he drove up the mountain to Ratón Pass and put the last few miles of Colorado behind him, he began to see cars with road ice bearded behind the tires and along the bottom. Almost all the cars had their lights on. He began to wonder if he would make it to Albuquerque the first day, and he hoped he didn't have to spend the night in Ratón. He had stayed there once, after coming down the mountain in a snowstorm and finding the highway closed. The next morning in the coffee shop, he overheard chatter about "black ice" parties, which he understood to mean local people getting drunk with stranded travelers, and he didn't think he had missed much.

Down the hill as he came to the first off-ramp for Ratón, he tried to gauge the road ahead. It was about a hundred miles to Las Vegas, New Mexico, a pit of a town for travelers, at least. Snow was falling, about an inch of it so far on the side of the road, and he had at least three hours of daylight driving. He looked at the gas gauge. He had filled up in Pueblo, and he still had plenty. Even though he was in no hurry, he figured the farther he could go the first day, the better he would like it. At the second off-ramp he looked at the tall signs advertising gas stations, hamburger chains, and motels, and he drove on, his tires whispering in the slush.

Snow began to pile up as he drove south. He slowed to fifty-five, then forty-five, then thirty-five. Most of the traffic kept to the right lane now, in caravan style, following a wide set of tracks on the packed snow. From time to time a fearless driver would blow by on the left. Clark stayed in his place, trying to relax in the slow, quiet pace but feeling the tension every time he saw a set of brake lights come on.

An hour rolled by, and then another. Clark saw one car and then a second one pulled off to the side with lights flashing. A couple of minutes later he saw a mid-sized grey car that had slid off the road. It was down in a flat area, where two long-haired kids were pushing and rocking it while a third one spun the tires. As nearly as Clark could tell, the road had not iced up yet, but it was slippery and he imagined it would freeze after nightfall.

Clark hit the button to find a new station. He heard a commercial for a car dealer back in Ratón, which made him feel he hadn't gotten that far down the road. The recorded voice was full of energy, saying come on in and visit with the sales team, take advantage of the rebate, be assured that the warranty is backed up by the service team.

Clark hit the button again. Everyone had a team these days. Even the announcer on Sunday afternoons closed with best wishes from Billy Graham and the team. At work, the daily e-mail memos were full of the team rah-rah, praising the custodial team for setting up display tables, citing the management team or the planning team or the assessment team for making the commitment. What used to be a committee or a task force was now a team, and the good employees were team players. Clark thought the team philosophy might be a trickle-down cliché from the corporate world; he had read about Wal-Mart employees, dressed in their blue outfits, watching motivational videos and giving team cheers. He imagined the cliché was something people thought they were supposed to say because it sounded so purposeful when they heard it. When it came around to him at work, the sub-text was, don't bother with individual achievement, or at least don't expect to be recognized for it. Doing something for oneself was The Secret Life, cheating on the team. Maybe Flagstaff was the same way, but it was worth a look.

Whenever he was bombarded with the team philosophy, he couldn't help remembering there were a few things a person had to do alone—think, speak for oneself, have a relationship, have sex, take the consequences for any of it, and die. A guy didn't have sex all alone, but he had it on his own, without the team. And when it came time to die, some or all of the health management team might be on hand, but a person still had to go it alone.

Clark wondered if team players lived longer than others, if they were the kind he had heard about a few days earlier. The way it went was that a person who had a good childhood, lots of friends, and a good marriage relationship tended to have a longer life. Such a person had better blood pressure, cholesterol readings, and blood sugar metabolism. The way the announcer read it off, it sounded as if the factors were all things a person could have chosen to begin with or could have selected along the way, like what color to paint the house. But when Clark heard that blithe piece of wisdom, it made him think of how much of his life was already in the bag.

Dusk was drawing in, grey behind the white, as he drove along the old highway and main street of Las Vegas. It looked as if the town was already filling up with ice-crusted vehicles, so he decided to find a place to stay and then worry about what to eat.

He ended up in a room that he could just as well have found in any of the other half-dozen old motels along the strip. It had a dim overhead light, a wall furnace, cinder-block walls painted to look like wallpaper, a chest of drawers with a cracked formica top, a matching table that held the television and a microwave, and a bed with one thin blanket and a thinner bedspread. The bathroom was cold but clean, lined with old tile work in sections of light green, sky blue, aqua, salmon, and pale yellow. To the left of the sink, a bottle opener was screwed into the wall.

Clark turned on the television to see if he could find a weather report, but the closest he came to it was a newscast. He saw some footage taped earlier, in the daylight. An eighteen-wheeler had tipped over and scattered fresh fruit all over the median—small heaps of red apples, bunches of yellow bananas, netted bags of oranges. The reporter on the scene, an Hispanic woman in dark coat and gloves, said no one was allowed to pick up the fruit, for insurance reasons, and all the spilled produce would go to waste.

That was another kind of teamwork. Too bad things had to be that tight-ass, but the good old days weren't likely to come back. Like the time years ago when, on his way to work with the construction crew on a summer morning, he had seen a truckload of frozen chickens spilled all over the highway. Later in the day, when he and his pals stopped to buy beer on the way home, they heard that passersby had been allowed to pick up hundreds and hundreds of frozen chickens. One guy had put a huge pile of them in the back seat of an old Buick, as the story went. Clark had thought about those chickens a thousand times, how the truck had split open and scattered the shiny lumps, spreading out the opportunity for anyone who happened by.

A real team would be out there right now, in the cold, salvaging the apples and oranges, hustling to get things picked up before the temperature dropped too low, and trucking the fruit to the homeless shelters in Albuquerque. It was a dumpster diver's dream, but it was beyond anyone's individual effort. The whole mess was going to go to waste out on the frozen interstate, to be scooped up by a front loader, along with snow and mud and stray plastic pop bottles. Clark shut off the television, checked the thermostat on the wall heater, and went out to find a place to eat.

A waiter with earrings, a pigtail, and shaved temples served him a chili burger that he thought he might regret, then followed it up with a three-dollar error on the bill. Clark stood outside on the sidewalk and wavered, wondering whether to go back to his room. As if he needed one more bit of proof that Las Vegas was a seedy, tacky town, he went half a block down the hill and dropped into a tavern.

Half a dozen patrons in a row turned to look at him and then went back to watching the television on the wall. The woman behind the bar sat on a stool with her back to the cash register. She had shoulder-length, mouse-colored hair and a poochy stomach that sat in her lap. Clark figured her to be in her late thirties.

She held her elbow aloft as she took a puff on her cigarette. "I'm pullin' four tens on my day job and then workin' in here on the weekends. I mean, I don't have *time* for an affair. Least of all with you." She huffed out the last of the smoke and turned to Clark. "What can I getcha, hon?"

"Bottle of Michelob."

"Got no Mick. Bud all right?"

"Sure."

The television at the end of the bar had a basketball game in progress. The other patrons all had their backs to Clark and their heads tipped up to watch the game. The woman set the bottle of beer in front of him, took his five-dollar bill, and turned toward the cash register. She paused to answer a comment from the man she had been bantering with earlier.

"Not on your best day, Robby."

When she brought the change, Clark asked her if she knew whether the truck turn-over had been north or south of here.

"I've got no idea, hon."

"I'm goin' to Albuquerque in the morning, and I hope the roads aren't too bad."

She shrugged.

"Do they have black ice parties here?"

"I don't know what that is. And I don't have time for parties." She went back to her stool and picked up her cigarette. The man named Robby said something to her, and she answered, "Sounds like you ought to go on a blind date. And you know what kind I mean." The man said something else, and she quipped, "One of these days someone's goin' to jap-slap you."

A ripple of laughter went down the bar, and then everyone merged back into the basketball game. Clark drank his beer and wished he could listen to the jukebox instead. An image rose up in shadow, and he brushed it away. Delia misery.

* * * * *

By the time he got to Santa Fe the next morning, the roads were dry. As he drove along the Río Grande north of Albuquerque, the sun was shining. He imagined the highway would be clear on the way to Flagstaff, but he wondered if he should pull into a truck stop and ask. He figured he could get to Flagstaff by early evening if he didn't have any delays, but now he could feel hesitation lurking. Before he left home, he imagined a relaxed Sunday evening there—checking into a hotel, having dinner, going out for a couple of drinks. Now it was stacking up as a repeat of last night, with Sunday drunks to boot.

He saw fruit trees blooming in the back yards of some of the houses in Río Rancho. Probably peach trees, maybe some apricots, from the looks of them. Trees like those would be blooming all along the valley, on down to Socorro and Las Cruces. He had seen them the year before at this time, when he rode with Lennis.

He wondered if he should find a truck stop, and then he decided he didn't need a reason for not going to Flagstaff. If he didn't want to, he could just do something else—like take a dog-leg and head down to Ciudad Juárez. It was about the same distance, maybe even a little less. And he remembered something he had seen there.

When he came to the intersection of I-25 and I-40, he passed up the off-ramp that would have taken him to Gallup and beyond. As he followed I-25 out of Albuquerque, he felt his spirits lift. To hell with Flagstaff. This was his trip.

About twenty blocks from downtown Juárez, he looked for the hotel where he and Lennis had stayed, but he could not find it. He found another one that measured up just as well, so he pulled in. It was called the Villa Manport. It had a restaurant and bar as well as clean tile floors and a well-lit lobby. He paid for his room in dollars, got change in pesos, and had the good feeling that he was across the border.

As he was getting settled in the room, he noticed the bathroom had tile such as he had seen the evening before, except that it was all a pale custard color. A bottle opener was mounted on the face of the washstand, and on the counter sat two bottles of Peña Fiel mineral water. The place was clean, with a strip of paper wrapped around the toilet seat and lid, and little pink packets of soap labeled Rosa Venus.

On his way out to the street, he handed the key to the desk clerk and took a book of matches that had the hotel's name and address. On the tile steps outside, a cab driver asked him if he would like to go somewhere.

"*El centro*," he said. Downtown.

Some cars on the boulevard had their lights on, but night had not yet fallen. The driver did not speak until he pulled onto the main street in the downtown area. He asked Clark where he wanted to go.

"Right here is fine." He paid the cabbie, got out, and stepped up onto the sidewalk. The night was warm, in comparison with places up north, and people were wearing long-sleeved shirts or light jackets.

Doormen hailed him in English, and he peeked into a couple of night clubs. In each of them, an exotic dancer was gyrating around a brass pole. Clark walked down the street and passed a few more places that looked the same. Then he turned left, crossed the street, and went a block past the main drag.

A cab driver who was leaning against the front fender of his taxi asked him in Spanish if he was looking for girls.

"Do you know where they are?"

"Oh, yes."

"Here?" Clark looked around.

"There are a few on the street, but they are not very good."

"Oh."

"I can take you to a place where there are several, very pretty. You pick the one you like."

"I understand. How far?"

"Not very far. I can take you there in five minutes, and if you don't like it, I can bring you back."

"How much?"

"Four dollars."

It was the same amount he had just paid the other *taxista*. "All right. I'll take a look at it."

The man stood up and opened the passenger's door. He was a large man, with a flowery shirt hanging loose over his stomach. When he got in behind the wheel, he smiled at Clark and said, "This is a good place. You'll like it."

"Good. What is it called?"

"The Four Roses," he said in English.

"*¿Cuatro Rosas?*"

"Four Roses. Everyone says it in English." The driver turned right on the main drag, went four blocks, and turned right again. "Over here on the west side," he explained, going back to Spanish but saying "west side" in English, "there are some good places." He went three blocks, turned left, went a couple of blocks, and turned right.

He drove another block and was just pulling out of a stop sign when a large car materialized on the left and slammed into the taxi just in front of the driver's door and spun around parallel. It was a gunboat of an old Dodge, grey and white, with a lean man in a straw cowboy hat at the wheel. A girl about ten years old was sitting wide-eyed in the passenger's seat.

Clark was sure the other car hadn't had its lights on, and he assumed it had run a stop sign, but he couldn't see past the Dodge to be sure. At any rate, it was a genuine T-bone, and everything had come to a stop.

The taxi driver got out and walked to the window on the near side of the other car, which was the passenger's side. The window was open where the girl sat. After exchanging a few words with the man in the hat, the cab driver reached inside across the front seat and pulled the keys out of the Dodge.

Clark had the sinking feeling that something might happen, but the other driver just sat there and said something in a tone of self-defense.

It looked as if the taxi was going to be tied up for a while, so Clark got out and walked around the front of the car. He handed a five-dollar bill toward the taxi man, who frowned and shook his head. Clark thanked him and set out on foot.

So much for the Four Roses, at least for the time being. Dusk was falling, and Clark decided he would do best by heading toward the familiar downtown area, where there were street lights, women on the sidewalks, and other taxis if he wanted one. The collision had given him a surprise, followed by a chill, so he walked at a brisk pace to build up the fire again.

By the time his warmth had come back, he could see he was approaching the area he had in mind. He found a street that lay two blocks west of the main street and ran parallel to it. Following it to within a few blocks of the border, which he could see because of the levee and bridge, he came to an area of back-street bars, cafés, and hotels. In the dark doorway of a night club he saw two young and tawdry-looking women, not much more than girls, with too much lipstick and not enough flesh on their bones. He passed them by in favor of two others sitting in chairs on the sidewalk up ahead.

They hailed him as he walked by, and when he paused and asked them what was up, they launched into a frank conversation about what they would do and for how much. Both women were under thirty, he guessed. One was tall and slender with medium-length hair, while the other was of average height and a bit heavy, with her hair piled up on her hair. The tall one chewed gum, and the heavy one smoked a cigarette. They told him he could go to the room with whichever one of them he chose, or he could go with both. They had a jaded air about them, and in spite of their showing a great deal of leg and shoulder, Clark did not feel inspired.

He went down the block, crossed over, and walked back in the direction he had come from. Up ahead he saw a woman in a short orange dress. She was sitting on a window ledge with her legs angling down in front of her. She wore hoop earrings and dark red lipstick. As Clark approached her, he felt no excitement, so he just nodded and walked past her.

Two blocks later he ran out of establishments, so he turned right and followed the sidewalk on an uphill climb. At the first corner, he looked to his right. A block away, on the other side of the street, three women were standing near a car. He crossed the street, turned right, and headed toward them.

As he came close, the woman closest to him, who was leaning against a car, stood up straight. She looked to be in her late thirties and holding up well, as her figure was trim in a tight short outfit, all black. The other two women looked much younger, perhaps in their early twenties, and they stood off the sidewalk behind the end of the car.

"*Hola, güerito,*" said the older woman. Hello, whitey. "What's going on?"

"Nothing."

"What are you looking for?"

"Oh, who knows? I'm just looking around." He glanced at one of the younger women, and she smiled. The other one had her head turned away.

"What do you like?"

"I like girls."

"That's good. You have it all, right here."

He let his eyes rove across the younger one, who was wearing a light blue pullover sweater and a pair of white jeans. She wasn't showing as much as the others he had seen, and he figured she wasn't as seasoned. He turned his gaze back to the woman in black. "Are you all from the same place?"

"Yes." She glanced at a building that butted up to the sidewalk.

"Do these girls go to the room, too?"

"Just ask them."

"There's no problem if—"

She frowned and shook her head. "No, not at all. You ask the one you like the best, and she'll tell you."

He turned to the girl in blue and met her eyes. "What do you think? Do you go to the room?"

She moved toward the sidewalk as the other girl drifted away. "Yes. I go."

Clark took a couple of steps in her direction so he wouldn't have to speak so loud. "You go with me?"

She nodded, and he liked the movement of her long, dark hair.

"How much?"

"Two hundred pesos."

"Twenty dollars?"

"Yes."

"And how do we do it?"

"Regular."

At that moment, a man came out the door of the building. He had slicked-down hair, a thin mustache, and a short-sleeved white shirt. He said something to the older woman, and she gave him a short answer. The man turned and walked past Clark, gave a cross look at the girl in blue, and went back inside.

"Regular," said Clark, meeting her eyes again. "Do you take your clothes off?"

She gave a shrug. "*Sí, cómo no*." Yeah, why not.

Clark felt a surge, something he had been missing earlier. "That sounds fine. Shall we go?"

She nodded as before and led the way to the door. Once inside, she stopped at an open room and spoke to a frazzled woman who looked like the housekeeping staff. The old woman handed her a rolled-up towel and said something. The girl turned to Clark and said, "Give her the money."

He took out his wallet and gave a twenty to the woman. She took it, then with a hard look said, "Two more."

"What for?"

"For a small cooperation."

He plucked out two dollars and gave them to her, then followed the girl down a hallway.

She led him into a small room that had a dim light, a bare dresser, and a bed with a drab bedspread.

He watched her as she sucked in her stomach and unbuttoned the jeans. "Shall I help you take off your clothes?" he asked.

"I can do it. Take off yours."

He had them shucked in an instant and crawled under the bed cover. She unrolled the towel and handed him the foil package. Then she finished undressing and crawled in with him. She had a soft, wrinkled midsection but an otherwise firm young body, and she was not stingy with it. He imagined she hadn't been at this work very long, or she wouldn't have seemed to think it was so much fun.

When they were done and she was putting her clothes on, he asked her what her name was.

"Alma."

"Do you ever go to the U.S.?"

"No, I don't have papers."

"That's too bad."

She was straightening a barrette and looking in the mirror when he finished dressing.

"Here," he said, holding her a folded five-dollar bill. "This is for you. Don't give it to that nasty old man."

She rested her dark eyes on him and smiled. "Thank you." Then she tucked the bill into the tight front pocket of her jeans.

"Do you think I'll see you again?"

"I don't know."

"Are you going back outside?"

"Not right now. You go."

"Can I wait for you there?"

"No. He gets mad."

"That's all right. Will you be here tomorrow?"

"Probably not for a week."

Clark nodded and walked out the door, then down the hallway and out onto the street. The woman in the black outfit did not look at him until he paused by her.

"Do you know that girl Alma very well?"

She shook her head. "No, she just came here."

"Will she be here tomorrow?"

The woman raised a cigarette she had been holding out of sight. "I don't know."

Clark heard the door open, and he turned to see the man in the slicked-down hair. He looked at the woman and said, "Thank you. See you later." Then he walked away, in the direction of the border.

At the corner he turned right, then went a block and turned left, heading north again. Two blocks later he found a quiet-looking *cantina* where two women were tending a horseshoe-shaped bar. Clark noticed a couple of men drinking quart-sized bottles of beer, so he ordered one, calling it a *botella grande*, or large bottle.

"*Una caguama*," said the woman behind the bar.

She brought a *caguama* of Carta Blanca, like the other men were drinking. She asked for twenty-six pesos, so Clark paid with the change he had gotten at the hotel.

He looked at the label and saw that the bottle held a liter. He poured a glassful and took a long drink. It quenched his thirst, soaking into his tissues, and he felt the release spreading.

Alma. She was a good girl. New to this business and might not even be at it for long. He wished he had given her one of the slips of paper he had made up for Flagstaff, in lieu of a business card, but he doubted she would have called, much less send him an e-mail. She did her part, and even though there seemed to be a spark of actual friendship, she wouldn't have a reason to carry it any further. From the little contact Clark had had with that kind of woman in the past, it seemed as if they saw it all as a fair exchange and that was that.

Maybe she wasn't altruistic, but she had been cheerful and had done him some good. He filled the glass and took another drink. None of this was for the team.

He hadn't felt so free of tension in a long time. He remembered feeling this way one time a couple of years earlier, when he had cut through a snowdrift on the lane leading to his place. The wind had packed the snow hard, and he worked for two hours carving out the white slabs from the thickest part of the drift. After that he put the pickup in four-wheel drive and punched through the lower-lying stretch on the other side of his excavation. When he had broken a trail and driven over it a couple of times, he got out to load up the tools. The wheels were packed with snow, and water was dripping from the front fender wells. The sun was going down in a flame of red and yellow, and the meadowlarks were tinkling. A burden had lifted.

That was a bad winter. Things had shut down with Delia, and there had been a couple of bad accidents when the roads got icy. All of that seemed like a long ways away now, especially on this side of the border where some things were done with different protocol. On the other hand, none of it was ever very far away at all.

He pictured Alma again. He knew that she and Delia weren't the only two options in life, but he would take what he had right now. He felt the relaxation settling in, warm as a campfire and silent as frost.

Hunting Along the Wall

The alarm clock rang so sharp and clear that Clint could envision the little hammer striking the twin brass bells. In the darkness of early morning, in the cold of the high country, he did not even want to open his eyes, much less leave the warm sleeping bag. But he had to. With the first ringing of the hollow bells he felt the importance of getting up to hunt, and he reached his hand out into the cold to still the hammer. With his eyes open but without seeing the clock, he found and nudged the little lever that would hold the hammer in place.

His surroundings came back to him now—the warmth of the sleeping bag, the mixed smell of dust and pine, the tick-tick of the clock. From the other end of the tent came the sound of a man breathing in his sleep—it was Cody, where he had rolled out his bedding the night before. Clint couldn't see him, but he had a sense of the other man's presence. It was not an agreeable feeling, but rather a displeasure at having to bring along someone he wouldn't have invited as his first choice. Hunting was supposed to be an adventure, serious and fun, but this time it was cloyed with the obligation of getting his brother-in-law hunted.

Across the thin, cold air came a more pleasant sound now, the breathing of the horses. Clint felt the presence of the two animals standing outside the tent, a few yards away in their rope corral. The animals moved, and Clint could hear the muffled thud of the hooves. The sound brought the image of hard, dry earth. The first snow was yet to come, the snow that would put animals on the move and bring happiness to a hunter's heart.

But until the snow came, it was a dry world, hard and cold. Clint did not want to get up, but his pride moved him—pride of not being lazy, pride of doing the necessary tasks while his sister's husband stayed bundled in bed, pride of being up and out on the hunt before the sun came up.

He hadn't been out many times with Cody, but it was understood that Clint would get up first. It was fitting anyway, as Clint was more or less the guide on an excursion like this, being the owner of the tent and all the gear. Cody brought only his clothes, his bedding, his knife, his rifle, and the desire to kill animals.

Clint opened the zipper on his sleeping bag, unfolded the pants he had tucked inside, and put them on. Then he put on a thick cotton shirt over the thermal undershirt he had slept in. It was too dark to see colors, but he could feel the soft thickness of the cotton. Next he pulled on a wool jacket, still warm from having served as a pillow. He stood up, tucked in his shirt, and buttoned up his pants. He already had on his wool socks, from having slept in them. Now he put on his boots and wool cap, picked up his shaving kit, opened the flap of the tent, and stepped out.

It was a dark, still morning, certain and assuring. Pale moonlight struggled through a cloud cover. During the week, Clint had kept watch on the crescent moon as it grew from a sliver to a quarter moon. A brighter moon was not good for hunting because it helped animals stay out and feed at night; this moon, especially with the light cover, was all right.

After he had brushed his teeth, Clint put on his gloves and tended to the horses. He lifted a bag of alfalfa pellets from the horse trailer and carried it to the rope corral in the little stand of aspens. As he came closer, one of the horses whickered. Clint picked out the dark mane of the bay and spoke back. “Hey, Pepper.” Then he poured pellets into the two feed trays that lay just inside the corral.

The horses went to eating right away, and Clint stooped to pass through the ropes. He patted each horse as he spoke in a low voice. The rubber water basin was empty, so Clint shook it for debris and went for water. He poured most of a five-gallon can into the trough, then put away the water can and the feed sack. Still with no sense of time pressing, he crawled into the corral again and patted the horses. He felt the radiant warmth as it passed through his gloves, and he smelled the rich aroma of chewed alfalfa. These were the fine moments of early morning, the parts he liked to remember for the rest of the year.

Clint left the horses and went back to the tent. He lit the propane lantern, and the little world inside the canvas walls came alive, including the still form in the sleeping bag. Clint lit one burner of the gas stove, and for a moment he admired the blue flame before he filled the coffee pot and set it on the stove. While the water heated, he sorted out his gear. He stocked his vest with gloves, watch, license, and twine, then set the vest on the floor of the tent. He filled a quart bottle with water and stored it in the vest, and he felt satisfied that everything was in order.

When the coffee pot began to perk, Clint woke his brother-in-law. The lantern and the stove had cut the worst of the chill, and realistically, there hadn't been any good reason for the other man to get up until now anyway.

As usual, Clint made a breakfast of granola cereal, milk, and coffee. Cody, in spite of his slowness at coming out of his nest, didn't complain about anything. He dressed in a couple of minutes and took his seat in the camp chair, where he poured milk into his cereal. Then he poured his coffee and sipped it.

"Coffee's good," he said.

"Oh, yeah. It always is, in the mountains. It could taste like mud, and it would still be good."

"But it's good."

"Yeah, it is."

After he had eaten and had drunk his second cup of coffee, Clint put on his vest. He took out his watch and looked at it. It was almost five-thirty. He showed the time to Cody.

The brother-in-law nodded and spoke. "Anything with horns, right?"

"Yeah."

They had already covered the topic the night before, but it was normal to go through it again before going out, just to clarify. Clint preferred that each of them hunt for his own animal, but Cody liked the partner system—if one of them were to see two legal animals, he would try to kill both. Or, if only one hunter had a permit left, the two men would hunt until they filled it. Party hunting, it was called. Cody had pushed his preference the evening before, and now he was confirming it.

He must have sensed some reluctance, though, for he came back to the topic in his own way. "Look, if the chance comes up, kill two. I'm not here to look for a trophy, like I told you. I'm here for the meat, and your sister'll give me hell if I come home without any venison."

"That's fine, but I like it better if each guy kills his own. If we have to do it some other way, especially at the end of our stay here—well, fine, we can do it that way."

"Don't be sentimental. If you see a pair of 'em, shoot."

Clint hesitated. It seemed like a tactic on Cody's part, to offer his own permit in a selfless gesture in order to get Clint to agree again. "Okay," he said.

"Good." Cody drank from his coffee cup. "I'd better be gettin' ready. You're gonna get the horses, aren't you?"

"Sure." Clint zipped up his vest and ducked out of the tent. While he saddled the horses, he thought through the situation. His idea of hunting was more than an escape. It was part of a way of life—the real thing. A guy tried to do as much for himself as he could, in the basic tasks of life. Clint liked to raise a garden, gather wild fruit, raise calves, and bring in wild meat. Hunting was a piece in the larger order of things, and it had its own integrity.

It was important for him to do it all himself—find the animal, kill it, dress it, skin it, cut it up, and wrap it. He didn't need a butcher in his plan. Nor did he need someone else to squeeze the trigger, a minor but integral part of the larger scheme. For some hunters, pulling the trigger was a major part, the big thrill, and afterwards it was a matter of obligation to see to it that the meat didn't go to waste. And some of them, like Cody, talked about the meat in the time-honored manner as a way of justifying the bloodshed.

With the two horses saddled and tied off, Clint opened the pickup door to take out his rifle. He checked it to make sure it was unloaded; then he tucked it into the scabbard on the sorrel horse. He untied the two animals and led them to the front of the tent.

"All set, Cody."

"Okay. I'm coming." The light went off inside the tent, and the brother-in-law stepped out. "It's cold," he said.

"Yeah."

While Cody went to the cab and took out his rifle, Clint checked and tightened the cinches. They had a tendency to loosen up after the first few steps, when an animal relaxed.

The two men mounted up and left camp. They followed a trail that was barely visible in the faint light of the moon, but the horses knew the trail from the year before. The sorrel that Clint rode liked to keep a little ahead of the bay, which in a sort of tacit agreement stayed by the sorrel's side but half a length behind. The hooves of the two animals made a melody in the cold morning air. *Tlick-tlock, tlick-tlock, tlick-tlock, tlick-tlock*. The sorrel gave a snort, and the bay shook his bridle; but apart from those sounds, Clint heard only the rhythm of hooves striking the hard earth.

The trail made a slight climb, and after ten minutes the hunters had left the pines and had entered a broader country, a landscape of grass, sagebrush, and cedar. Now Clint could smell the dry grass, and the scent stirred him. The combination of smells—of cold air, dry grass, dust, and sagebrush—evoked a sense of the purity he was after. Horse, deer, earth, water, and stone. Rock didn't give off a scent, but it was part of the world he wanted to move in.

He was riding toward a formation called the Wall, so named because it was a long crest of rock—tall, narrow, and straight. It slanted off to the right from the top of the ridge the two men were climbing.

In the morning the deer would be along the base. One hunter would go along each flank of the wall, stepping soft, waiting, and moving on.

Despite its name, the wall was not a solid mass of rock. It had its cracks and clefts, its turrets and parapets, and once in a while a fugitive cedar growing in a cranny. At some points the deer crossed over through passageways, and for that reason it was good to have a man on each side, deaf and mute to the movements of the other, but ready.

They left the horses at the top, where Clint slipped off the bridles, put on halters, and tied the animals with lead ropes. The two men pulled out their rifles and moved away from the horses. Cody gave the signal of good luck and then headed down the left side of the wall.

Clint paused for a moment to tune into his surroundings. There was no wind. Dawn was coming. In the greyish light he could see rocks and cedars scattered across the landscape that opened up below him. He could see the first pink light in the east.

With his bare hand, Clint took out six cartridges from his vest. They felt heavy and cold, and as he looked at the pale brass casings he sensed the lethal aspect of the shells. He thumbed them into the magazine of the rifle, put on his glove, and went down the right side of the wall.

After dropping down the first slope, Clint paused. He stood motionless, absorbing the world again. The silence filled in around him. Dawn was opening now, off to his right, while the rock wall rose on his left. Minute by minute the objects in his field of vision became more distinct. He raised his rifle and looked through the scope. The clear view told him it was light enough to shoot, so he lowered the rifle, checked the safety, and moved on.

He walked without hurry, treading a few minutes and then stopping, looking around, listening, and moving on. In the first hour he spooked a jackrabbit and nothing more. He looked at it through the scope at a hundred yards, and his aim was steady on the animal as it sat motionless with its ears erect. Clint relaxed his hold on the rifle, and the jackrabbit took off.

After the second hour, during which time he had seen no animals at all, he saw a stain on the very base of the wall. He dropped into a squat as he took a studied look. It was a deer with its head down, grazing. Clint could see the left flank and the rear haunches, grey fading into saffron. He felt his heart-beat pick up, so he took a deep breath.

With his left elbow on his knee, he raised the rifle into position and looked through the scope. He still couldn't see the head. He relaxed and then focused another look. Now the deer raised its head and moved to the left, giving more of a profile. Clint made out the antlers, dull like dirty ivory in the dim morning light.

The deer was about two hundred yards away, quite a distance, without offering a good shot at the vital area. Clint let out his breath as he brought the rifle down. He knew he would have to get closer before he could shoot.

The deer turned its head and lowered it, then took a step. After a moment or so it moved forward again, and then again, until it disappeared behind a cedar.

Clint decided to wait a little while. With the rifle resting across his raised left knee, he took the quart water bottle out of his vest and drank about a fourth of the water. His mouth had gone dry, and the water helped settle him. He wet his lips and felt the water spread in his stomach. Then he put the water bottle back into his vest, picked up his rifle, and rose into a crouch. Making good note of the cedar and nearby rocks, he began his approach.

He took light steps and tried to keep objects such as rocks and bushes between himself and the spot where the deer had disappeared. He zig-zagged, taking it slow and trying not to attract attention. Within fifteen minutes he came to the spot without seeing any movement. He imagined the route that the deer must have taken, a trail that wound to the left through the sagebrush along the base of the wall. He was on the verge of following the trail when he heard a noise up above, the sound of a step or of a stone turning over.

Looking up and to the left, he saw the source of the noise. A deer, probably the same one from the looks of his antlers, was climbing along a ledge. The animal was making a steep climb, moving step by step without any hurry. It was about a hundred yards away, and forty or fifty feet higher than the ground level. Because of the distance, the deer didn't look very big as Clint swept it with the scope, picking up the left hindquarter first and then moving forward to the head.

Clint relaxed the rifle. The deer seemed unaware of the man, but it kept moving. Decided, Clint flicked the safety, raised the rifle, found the deer again in the scope, put the crosshairs behind the shoulder, and squeezed off a shot.

Without flinching, the deer gave a half-turn to the left and held still, showing more of its profile than before. Clint assumed he had missed, for if he had hit the deer, it would not have turned the way it did. It would have stiffened up, or it would have fallen. Instead it was keeping calm, now looking straight at the man below. Clint worked the bolt, ejecting the spent shell and jacking in a new one. Wavering a little, he put the crosshairs on the dark chest and fired again.

He expected to see the deer fall from the ledge, but the animal surprised him. With no great hurry but at a faster pace than before, it turned to the right, gave six or seven leaps up the trail, and disappeared in a passageway that no doubt crossed over the ridge. Clint was left with the image of a set of antlers, three points on each side, dancing with the wavy motion of the retreating deer.

Clint felt dazed for a moment. What had happened seemed unreal. The animal had been there, and then it was gone. As usual when he hunted, he had not heard the loudness of the shot nor felt the kick of the rifle butt. But it had happened, he knew that. He opened the bolt action and eased out the spent casing; then with a quick look he found the other one on the ground. He knelt to pick it up. With the rifle upright in his left hand, he studied the two empty brass cylinders in his right palm. He moved them with his thumb. He nodded. *Uh-huh, that's the way it was.* He stood up and put the two casings in his vest pocket.

With discouragement settling in, he continued his stalk along the base of the wall. He told himself he needed to stay alert; it was early yet, and the first day of the season. There was no reason to get too down on himself. It was just the elevation that caused him to miss. He was aiming way up high. He would have to think about that the next time, remember to adjust his aim.

He stood for a few moments in silence, then moved on. A couple of minutes more had gone by when he heard the crash of a shot, a sound that traveled along the other side of the wall. Cody had run into the deer.

After a long moment another shot came, and another, and then a fourth one. Then silence. Clint held still, listening. A guy couldn't tell with that many shots. Sometimes they came like that when the hunter missed one shot after another, especially if the animal was running.

A few minutes later, Clint heard the shout he had been waiting for. It was the clear sound of his own name. He looked up and back toward the place where the deer had disappeared, and there was Cody, waving at him from the top of the wall.

Clint made a fast climb to the top, and when he got there, Cody was exuberant.

"Well, we had some luck, man."

"Oh, really? You killed him?"

"Not just one, man. I killed two."

"Two? Really?"

"Yeah. The first one was a four-pointer, and then the second one was a three-pointer." Cody slapped his gloved hand on Clint's shoulder.

"So there were two, uh?"

"Yep. There were. When I heard your shots I got ready. You missed, didn't you?"

"Well, yeah." It occurred to Clint that if he himself hadn't missed, Cody could have killed an extra animal without knowing it, just for the sake of pulling the trigger on a nice animal.

"Well, I got ready, and pretty soon the big one came out, slow, and I knocked him down with the first shot. And then when his little brother came out, movin' a little faster, it took me three shots to put him down."

Clint nodded, then looked up at the sky. It was clouded over, but he could see the sun was still in the east. Just a few hours into opening morning, and someone else had already done his deer hunting for him. "It's early," he said. "We'll have plenty of time to get 'em both back to camp."

"Oh, yeah," Cody answered. He put his thumb under the sling strap on his shoulder, turned, and led the way down to the kill.

As usual, Clint did the bloody work. It was more convenient if only one person got bloody, and Clint preferred to do the job so that everything would come out clean and neat. Furthermore, he liked the work. He liked the challenge of doing it well, and he would just as soon not have someone else sticking his hands in the middle of it. He didn't know how Cody would do it, because whenever the two of them had gone out, Clint had tended to the dead animals. So now, in his double role of guide and gunbearer, he took out his clasp knife and went to work on the deer that had the most bullets in him.

As he opened the belly on the deer, Clint thought about how he wanted to do things. This far from camp or a vehicle, he preferred to field dress the deer and leave them splayed open until he could get back with the pack animals. He spoke his thoughts to Cody, who agreed. Then as he worked his way into the animal, he asked Cody to help from time to time by holding a leg and tipping the animal. Other than that, he did not speak.

In an hour, Clint had the two animals clean and split open, cooling in the autumn air. Cody poured water so he could scrub his hands. As Clint had said very little during the field dressing, he imagined his brother-in-law had gathered he wasn't very happy.

Cody still had a cheerful tone, though, when he spoke up. "We'll split the meat half and half, uh? That one's bigger, but since we did it on partners, we can split it even."

"Sure." Clint glanced at the two animals. "But you can keep the horns."

"Nah, man. That three-pointer's yours. I shot him for you."

Clint felt the anger spark up inside, but he restrained himself. Then, with what he hoped was a tone of finality, he said, “Look, I don’t want the horns. You killed ’em both, you keep all the horns. We’ll split the meat, and that’s that.”

Cody put up his hands. “That’s okay. I didn’t mean for you to get mad.”

“I’m not goin’ to be mad. But we’ll leave it at that.” He paused for a second and then said, “I’ll go get the horses.”

Cody glanced at the rifle leaning against a clump of sagebrush. “Are you gonna leave your rifle here?”

“I don’t have any reason to carry it up with me and then back down.”

Cody raised his eyebrows. “No, I guess not. Well, okay. I’ll wait here.”

With his gloves in the pouch of his hunting vest, Clint went back the way his brother-in-law had come. The trail made an uphill climb, and it gave him exercise. That was good for working off the anger.

Well, he thought, it could have been worse. His deer hunting was over for the season, but that was what he got for hunting with Cody to begin with and for agreeing so easily, or even at all, to hunt on the partner plan.

He put his hand in the right pocket of the vest and touched the two casings. In his mind he could see them, two empty pieces of brass.

He stopped and took a drink of water. Then he started back up the trail that would take him to the horses. They would be happy to see him.

Nice Boots

It's a pretty good rifle—Winchester .270, with a sling and a scope. I saw the guy in here one day, and we got to talking, and he asked me if I wanted to buy it. As it turns out, it might be the only thing that was legitimate about the guy.

I knew him because he was sort of a pal of my sister. She's a secretary at the college, you know, and he's one of the teachers. Or was. A bunch of them would go to happy hour together, over at the Top Hat Lounge, and he was never in any hurry to leave, so I've had a few drinks with him there. He's the type of guy that wears boots and creased Wranglers, and likes to talk about his hunting trips and his elk hunting horse and all that. He seemed all right, just to sit around and talk to him, and I'd see him in here once in a while, too.

He needed to sell this rifle because he'd fallen on hard times. I'd already heard his wife had given him his walkin' papers and he'd gotten bounced from his job. Didn't get re-newed for the next year. He had to leave town, I guess, and he was scraping money together to leave on. I imagine he had to sell his horse and trailer and all—probably his saddle, too. I knew he was up against it, so I offered him three and a half, and he took it. Not a bad rifle at all.

When I went over and picked it up, he told me there was a gun case that went along with it, but it was at his old lady's. Or ex-old-lady's. She'd gotten a divorce and ended up with the house. He was living in one of those little apartments behind Safeway, the type that the college students live in during the school year. I was wondering why he got canned, so I asked him if they were doing a down-sizing and he got caught in it. He said not as far as he knew. They just didn't renew his contract, and he didn't know why.

Funny stuff, really. The guy seems like a bad check, after you've known him for a while. Not that I knew him all that well. But you'd see him around town, in the coffee shops in the morning or maybe the bars in the afternoon, when everyone else would have been working. You wondered how he managed it, you know? But still, you get the impression that they have a hell of a time firing a teacher, unless he comes to work drunk all the time or they catch him nailing a student in his office. I mean, isn't that the way it seems to you? Anyway, I mainly knew him through my sister. He always acted like a good old boy, with pearly-snap shirts and nice boots. But like they say, you wonder if he ever had any shit on the outside of those boots, or if it was all on the inside.

So I bought the rifle from him and figured I'd call it good, and then I got a call from his wife. She said I could come and pick up the gun case. I figure what the hell, so I go over there, and she takes me through the house to the garage. I gather that she thinks I'm some kind of a hunting pal of old Doo-Fitchee, and I didn't really say anything to the contrary. Actually, though, the only time I ever ran into him hunting was one time out on some BLM land west of town, and he was letting his thirteen-year-old kid hunt on his antelope license. I don't know where the kid was when I went over for the gun case, though. He ought to be about sixteen or seventeen now, so he was probably off hot-rodding around.

She was just there by herself, you see, and she was wearing a pair of shorts and a skimpy blouse, and she's not all that bad-looking. Maybe a little chubby, but not bad. Anyway, she asks me if I'd like a cup of coffee, and then she starts flirting with me, and the next thing I know, we're sitting on the couch and she's practically in my lap. Things warm up pretty quick, and we end up in the bedroom. I mean, she just about pushed her boobs in my nose, and I had to defend myself. Jeez, what would you do? Well, I know what I did. It was right there on the plate, you might say.

So I don't see any more of this guy, but after a while I hear from my sister about how he got bounced from his job. It didn't come out right away, partly because the school year was over and not very many people were around, but eventually it turns out that his wife squealed on him for not doing his work. She handed over two boxes of tests and term papers and all, with not a mark on any of them. My sister says the students used to complain that they didn't get their work back from him. He'd say it was graded but it was at home. You think, what the hell is it doing at home if it's graded? But it wasn't. He just had it warehoused.

And you wonder how he figured grades for the kids. Did he just give 'em grades according to how well he liked them? Or did he have some kind of impression from what they did in class? From what I heard, he didn't even grade the little quizzes, where you check off true or false, you know, or mark a, b, or c.

I always wondered what those guys did to draw their pay. Not very much, from the sounds of it—some of them, at least. I wonder how in the hell he thought he could get away with it. Or better yet, why he couldn't get it together to do his work. What if you or I tried something like that? Like in your case, I'm guessing you can't charge someone for a new roof unless you put on some shingles. Tell me if I'm wrong. Same with me. If I go out to do a farm kill, I'd better come back with a slaughtered beef or hog or whatever in the truck, and if they put me in the cold room to grind meat, I'd better have a big pan of hamburger to show for it. Maybe he let the work pile up so much that he couldn't deal with it, so he just got in the habit of stashing it. But still, I mean, where's your pride?

So his wife turned in these two boxes of papers, saying they were the property of the students and should be protected. That was a nice move on her part. Of course, whoever was in charge just took the stuff and locked it up. It would have been a hell of a mess to let all those students know, and then have to re-figure grades for anyone that complained. Instead, it gave the bosses some pretty good leverage on him, so they were able to get him to hand in his keys without them having to do a thing. Once the word got around, I'd think it would have put him to shame with everyone he worked with. He'd probably want to leave anyway.

From what I heard, the wife said he had dumped tons of this stuff over the years and had told her not to breathe a word to anyone. I guess when she finally had enough of him and shoved him out, she figured this was a way to kick his ass but good. She had to be awfully pissed at him. Of course, I didn't know anything about this when I bought the rifle or went over to pick up the gun case. I heard it later from my sister.

What I don't get is why he hoarded the evidence. It's like the stories you hear about people who stack up dead cats in their freezer, or people who can't get it together to deliver the mail and then keep it all in a room in their house. You've heard those stories, haven't you? Years and years of junk mail—flyers and catalogues and the like—that they don't have the energy to deliver and don't have the brains to get rid of. I guess he threw out heaps of the stuff in the past, but he must have had a couple of years' worth in the boxes she turned in.

I probably would have bought the rifle even if I'd known what a phony he was. I mean, it was a good deal. But my sister isn't taking it so well. He just skipped out on her, and left her in the lurch. The people at work are giving her the "I-told-you-so" treatment. Same old story, you know. Wait till the guy gets busted, and then everyone says they knew he was a flake all along. Which is embarrassing to her, of course.

The guy's wife has tried to make her look like a home-wrecker, on top of that. All it takes is one or two trips to the beauty shop, and it's out on the street that Rhonda is the other woman. It seems like the guy's wife has it in for her pretty bad and wants to spite this guy any way she can. So she bad-mouths Rhonda and makes her look like a fool as well.

She didn't say anything to me about it. I don't know if she even knows I'm Rhonda's brother or if she just thinks I'm some pal of her husband's. Either way, I haven't been back for seconds. It was good sex, you understand, but when I called her back, she wasn't interested. I imagine once was enough for her.

I can't help feeling sorry for my sister, even if she got herself into it. I used to tell her not to go out with cowboys, because they were so likely to just take what they could get. Hell, I remember one time, when she was barely old enough to go out to the bars, and I wasn't much older. She told me about this one cowboy who was telling his friends he took her home with him. So I went up to the kid, grabbed him by the front of his shirt, and told him if he said anything like that again I'd knock his teeth out. Then her new boyfriend, who was also a cowboy, told me it was true, that the other guy did take her home, but he—that is, her new boyfriend—wasn't mad about it, because she wasn't sleeping with the other guy any more.

Well, hell. There's only so much you can do for your sister. But it seems like she would have been just as well off to marry some cowboy and get divorced from him, rather than get tangled up with some phony sonofabitch like this guy. Jeez-Marie, it's no wonder his wife booted his ass out.

Chokecherries Are Free

Alan brought the maul down hard, splitting the length of firewood into two halves. He set up another piece, hefted the maul, and swung it down again. The wood did not split all the way this time. Alan pulled the head of the maul out of the crack where it was wedged, set up the round again, and cleaved it with another hard, fast stroke.

He looked up and around at Todd, who was filling the afternoon with the racket of the chain saw as he cut the large branches into stove lengths. Todd didn't seem to mind the noise of the saw, even up close, as he triggered the engine and sank the teeth into the dry wood.

Alan glanced behind him at the wood he had split and kicked aside. He and Todd had well over a cord cut by now. It would make a good stack, all neatly cut with the yellow ends sticking out. He looked again at Todd, who was just about finished cutting up the last tree. The branch fell apart as the bar of the chain saw dipped down and came back up. Todd moved a foot and a half to his right, poised the saw, triggered up the r.p.m.'s, and gouged the bar into the next cut.

Some guys were that way. They liked running a machine, even if it made their ears ring and shook the hell out of their hands. It gave some level of satisfaction—Alan was sure of that, even if he didn't feel it himself.

That was the way Todd had been at the job site, a few days earlier. He had an air of authority as he unchained the backhoe, dropped the ramps, fired up the engine, and backed the outfit off the trailer. With the same authority he jockeyed the backhoe into position, set down the hydraulic feet to stabilize the rig, and dug the iron claw into the ground. It was all matter-of-fact as the arm reached out, bit down, pulled closer, lifted, swung to the side, and released the load of dirt that came out of the trench. Alan glanced over from time to time as he nailed down floor decking.

When Todd finished digging the trench and had the backhoe chained onto the trailer once again, he came over to talk to Alan. Todd said he had just come back to town after being gone for a couple of years, and things had changed. Everyone was married now.

"How 'bout you?" he asked.

"Not right now," Alan answered.

That seemed to be enough to renew a friendship. Now they were cutting wood together, getting ready to stack it.

Alan split three more rounds until he had moved up the branch far enough that the wood didn't need splitting any more. The chain saw had finally quieted down, and Todd was smoking a cigarette, the sun brightening his blond mustache and glinting off his sunglasses.

Carrying the maul, Alan walked over to speak to Todd. "I imagine he's got a wheelbarrow around here somewhere."

Todd sniffed and turned down the corners of his mouth. "Nah, shit. We can just toss the pieces in the pickup, then stack 'em by the back door."

And so the job went. By three o'clock they had the wood stacked at the edge of the patio and were driving out to the main road.

Todd glanced in the rear-view mirror and said, "That should make Jay happy."

Alan said "Uh-huh" and looked in the mirror on his side. All he saw was the little stucco house.

On the way into town, Todd asked Alan if he would like to have a beer somewhere and watch a football game. Alan said he'd just as soon get home, so Todd left him off at the apartment.

Sheila sat up on the couch as Alan closed the door behind him. "Oh, hi," she said. "I didn't expect you home this soon."

"Yeah, we finished at about three, so I came on home."

She smiled. The afternoon daylight lit up the living room of the apartment, and Alan thought she looked pretty sitting there, with her glossy dark hair touching the slope of her bosom. She looked rested and happy, as her black-cherry eyes were shining.

She patted the couch with her left hand, so he sat down beside her. In a moment he had his arms around her and had met her lips in a kiss.

"Did you work hard?"

"Oh, yeah. Todd ran the chain saw, and I split the thicker pieces. Then we stacked it all."

"So everything worked out fine."

"Uh-huh. Todd says Jay doesn't hunt, so we'll get first crack at 'em next week."

"That's good."

"Yeah, these guys have a little circle, I guess, where they all do each other favors. Sort of a trade-off."

"Well, it's nice of Todd to cut you in, if that's what it is."

"I think so. He hasn't been back in town all that long, and I think he likes to have pals. He asked me if I wanted to go have a beer, but I told him I wanted to get home."

"You could have gone."

"Oh, I know. But I'd rather be here. I can drink a beer here, and not be missing a thing." He kissed her, then got up and went to the refrigerator. He took out a can of Coors, popped it, and walked back to the couch.

"Did he just want someone to drink a beer with, then?"

"I think so. He asked me the other day if I was married, and I said no. So I think he's lookin' for someone to buddy up with him and hit the bars and all that." Alan took a drink and sat down. "I didn't tell him I was living with you because I didn't think that was what he was asking."

"Oh, well, you can tell him later."

"Sure."

"I guess he *is* kind of looking around. Now that I think of it, I saw him the other day. It must have been Thursday. In the store. He said hello and gave me a good looking over, like he could tell I was preggers, and then he didn't pay any more attention."

"Oh. Did you, um, know him before?"

"I went out with him once or twice, before I married Randy, but it was nothing serious. And the other day, I just had the feeling that he was taking a look at everything."

"Sort of seeing what was on the market."

Sheila laughed. "Uh-huh. So he didn't waste much time on me."

Alan laughed with her. "That's good." He took another drink and put his arm around Sheila. "I think he's just trying to fit back in—you know, find out what circles he wants to move in."

"Were you pretty good friends before?" Sheila's voice carried a note of uncertainty.

Alan gave it a thought. "Oh, probably nothing special. Just normal kind of friends. We'd run into each other in the bars, maybe hit a few places together. But we didn't ever work together, or go on trips, or hunt together, or any of those things."

Sheila nodded. "I see."

"Like I say, I think he's just seeing where he fits. He's got his own truck and backhoe, so he's getting into that circle of guys. They send work to one another, and they go into cahoots on this thing or that."

Sheila frowned. "Like what?"

"Oh, nothing shady. Maybe he'll go dig a basement for some realtor who'll turn around and help him get into a house that the bank foreclosed on. Or maybe two of 'em 'll buy a piece of property, build on it, and sell it." Alan shrugged. "That sort of thing."

"So you didn't just go cut wood so you could hunt on this place that Jay bought."

"Well, I guess I did. I mean, I don't have a business, and I don't wheel and deal, so that's the only part I have in it. But Todd, he probably buys all his insurance through Jay, and next time he needs to buy something, he'll probably get the loan through Jay's brother-in-law, and so forth."

"Nice to have that sort of thing to worry about."

Alan widened his eyes. "I guess so." He thought for a second. "Actually, those guys really are in a different league. Like that one move they pulled, where they bought the farm land and then got it annexed. There was a controlled growth policy in effect, and they weren't supposed to be able to do that for another two years. But Jay's brother-in-law is on the city council, and I'm sure he helped push that through." Alan looked at Sheila and smiled. "I don't think we're missing much."

"I don't think so, either."

He took a drink of his beer. "I mean, so what if you have to live hand-to-mouth for a while. We're workin' on a plan, so what the hell. Let them go fishing in Mexico, or golfing in Arizona, or whatever they plan to do this winter."

Sheila wrinkled her nose and then smiled. "We'll just stay here and take care of the bun in the oven."

Alan set his beer on the coffee table, then placed his free hand on Sheila's stomach. "That's right. We're just getting started in the catalogue. We still have to order all the accessories."

She laughed. "What do you think we should work on next?"

"Well, we did the eyelashes last night. Maybe we could put in an order for fingernails."

Alan worked through the week at the job site. When he and Mike had run up all the walls, Mike brought in a third man to help them with the trusses. It was a straight, ranch-style house, with nothing fancy in the way of peaks or gables, so they got the trusses all nailed into place in one day.

The next morning, Thursday, brought the first frost of the season. The new lumber of the house frame sparkled with sunlight glancing off the white crystals. Mike and Alan worked on the ground as the frost faded from the rafters. They set up a pair of sawhorses and stacked the roof sheathing on them, with the sheets leaning against the eaves of the house, so they could pull the sheets up from the roof and nail them to the rafters. With the stacking done and the light frost just about gone on the sunny side of the house, they took a coffee break before going up onto the roof.

Mike told a story about a roofer who had slipped on a frosty roof in the early part of the fall, at about this time of year. He landed on both feet and broke his heels. It was a tough break for the fellow, Mike said. He had to go back to school, in his thirties, to learn how to do something else.

Alan nodded and looked around. This morning's frost was not lasting long, and sometimes the second frost didn't come for another week or ten days, but the idea was there all the same. The leaves would turn color, and cold weather would be on the way.

* * * * *

On Friday evening, Alan and Sheila sat down to a dinner of chuck roast with potatoes, carrots, and onions. Sheila looked pretty with her dark hair shining beneath the dining room light, and her eyes were soft. Alan felt happy—a little guilty at drinking a beer when Sheila couldn't, but happy at the thought of having a cozy meal and sweet company. There lived at the edge of his memory a long string of Friday nights that had begun with happy hour, stumbled through pizza or fast food or no food, and come to a blurry end at midnight or closing time. Friday nights had been that way before he got married, at times when he was married, and most of the time after he had gotten his divorce. He didn't miss all those Friday happy hours with their forced hilarity. He liked it here with Sheila.

She had set out a jar of chokecherry jelly that they had opened earlier in the week. For dessert they each buttered a slice of wheat bread and spread jelly on top. Sheila's eyes sparkled as she held up her bread and jelly in a salute with Alan's.

It came to him again, the memory of the day they had gone to pick chokecherries. It was mid-August, six weeks earlier. They drove up to the mountains to a place she knew, and after a picnic and then a nap in the camper, they picked the chokecherries. They had just found out she was pregnant, and she had moved into his apartment, waiting for her divorce from Randy. They didn't want to rush into getting married, and they weren't free to do so anyway, but life was free and open otherwise. They didn't have to answer to anybody, and the day was all theirs, a sunny, blue-sky day in the National Forest where the creek rippled and the chokecherries grew free under the open sky. To Alan it was the first memorable day of this happy time together.

The next day they cooked the chokecherries, squeezed out the juice, and made the jelly, putting it up in fourteen pint jars. Now they had the beginnings of a reserve, some version of a nest egg as they got ready for the winter and things that would come after that.

A deer would make a good addition to their stocking up. It would go a long ways through the months ahead. They had both said, more than once, that they hoped he got a deer. Now he said it again as they ate their bread and jelly, and she agreed.

In the morning, Sheila went with Alan as far as Todd's place so she would have the pickup for the day. Todd sat in his red Dodge pickup, warming the engine, as Alan pulled around the corner and parked across the street, facing the opposite direction. Leaving the engine running, Alan got out of the cab and gathered his rifle, vest, and day pack. As Sheila settled in behind the wheel, he kissed her good-bye. She wished him good luck, then rolled up the window and drove away. Alan crossed the street and got into the red pickup.

Todd looked in the rear-view mirror as he pulled away from the curb. "I thought you weren't married."

"Well, I'm not." Alan settled the pack on the floorboard between his feet. Then, so Todd wouldn't have to ask more questions, he added, "That was Sheila."

Todd seemed to take a moment to register what he had heard and perhaps to put it together with what he had seen before. "I thought she was married to Randy."

"Well, she was. Actually, she still is, but not for long."

"Oh."

The sky was just turning grey in the east when Todd turned off the county road onto Jay's property. He drove through the yard, which seemed as empty as before, and on north, through a cattle guard, and into a pasture that sloped upwards.

"The breaks are just up ahead." Todd clicked the gear selector into a lower gear.

Alan nodded and looked out into the dark morning. He had understood that the breaks sloped off to the west for a good half mile; if the deer were anywhere out here, Todd had said, they were likely to be in these gullies.

Alan stepped from the cab into the chilly air. Always coldest at daybreak, he thought as he put on his vest. He took gloves from the left pocket and put them on, then felt for his rifle shells in the right pocket. He lifted his rifle from the gun rack and closed the door, shutting off the flow of light on his side of the cab.

The grass was dry under his feet as he walked around the front of the pickup. Todd was wearing his own orange vest, bright in the light that came from the cab, and had slung his rifle over his shoulder. He closed the door of the pickup, then lit a cigarette in the grey light of morning.

"If you want to go down this one here, I'll go on up a ways and start down another one." The end of Todd's cigarette glowed, and a cloud of smoke came out onto the morning air. "I'd say, as soon as it's light enough to shoot, we start down. Take it slow, maybe an hour and a half to the bottom."

Alan yawned and nodded. They had already talked it over, but just to confirm, he said, "Then we hunt back up to the vehicle, right?"

"Unless we kill something. Then one of us can come back for the truck and drive down around to the bottom."

Alan nodded again, and the two of them wished each other luck. Todd moved away, letting out another puff of smoke.

Alan moved away from the pickup in the direction of the broken country. He took slow steps, giving Todd enough of a lead that they would start down at about the same time. He paused at the head of the gully. In a few more minutes, it would be light enough to hunt. This was a good moment—daybreak on opening morning, in good deer country, with private land all to themselves. He knew that a county road ran north and south along the bottom of the breaks, and he understood that the gate had a chain and padlock on it. It was nice to have the privilege, he thought, whether he got a deer or not.

The cool, dry air carried the scent of dirt, grass, and sagebrush—the smell of early autumn, deer season. He was glad he had come. He could have worked this day, but there would be plenty of days to work, and deer season lasted only two weeks.

He kept the rising sun at his back and moved in the shade when he could. He took it slow, expecting to see deer in the sunny spots, but he saw nothing larger than a cottontail. The sun rose and pulled the shadows in. A pickup rattled northward along the county road, but no other sounds broke the morning stillness.

At the bottom, Alan found Todd sitting against a windmill tank, smoking a cigarette.

"See anything?"

Alan shook his head.

"Me neither. I wonder if we chased any out."

Alan shrugged. "Hard to say. They may be off on someone's hay field, and come back here later to shade up."

Todd spit at the ground. "Could be. But I think this was the best bet." He stood up, dropped his cigarette butt, and ground it out with his bootheel. "Well, I guess we can hunt a couple more draws back up to the top."

Alan scanned the country as it rose before him. The red pickup was not visible from down below, but he knew where it was. If they moved north and hunted back up, they would come out about a quarter of a mile in front of the pickup.

Hunting uphill didn't seem like a very good prospect. Alan had a general sense that deer kept a better lookout below them than above, just as sounds traveled up more clearly than down. But the pickup was at the top, so it was just as well to hunt on the way back if they had to climb anyway. As he trudged up the draw, he wondered if there might be a better way to hunt this piece of country, maybe tomorrow morning. One fellow could hunt across the top while the other poked along the bottom. That would be an idea, at least.

He met Todd up on top as planned. They slung their rifles onto their shoulders and headed toward the pickup. Alan was about to mention his idea when a shot crashed below and rippled up through the breaks.

"I wonder if that's on our place." Todd unslung his rifle and jogged toward the head of the breaks.

Alan followed, bringing his rifle down and around as well, to keep it from banging on his shoulder. He ran the short distance and paused at the edge next to Todd. Down below, a dark pickup was pulled off the road on this side, and two men in orange vests were climbing over the fence.

"Sure as hell is on us," Todd said. "It looks like they shot something. We'd better get down there." He took off running towards the pickup.

Alan followed, reaching the cab in time to pile in as Todd gunned the engine.

It was a fast ride back down the pasture, through the cattle guard, across the ranch yard, onto the county road that led west, and then right onto the road that ran north.

The dark pickup was still off to the side of the road, and the two men in orange vests were dragging a deer toward the fence. It didn't look like a very large deer, but it had antlers big enough for each man to get a hand-hold, so it was legal. Shooting from the road, of course, wasn't—and neither was trespassing.

"God-damn road-hunters." Todd was digging a cell phone out of its case as he slid into a stop behind the dark blue Ford.

The two men had stopped in their tracks, still holding the buck by its antlers. It hung limp and loose, with its ears drooping.

Todd got out and laid his rifle across the hood, pointing off a little to the left of the two road-hunters. Alan could see their two rifles safely racked across the rear window of their cab.

"Just drag it up to the fence and leave it there," Todd called out. "I'll have someone here in a few minutes." He punched a few numbers into the phone, then spoke up again. "You might as well get over here."

The trespassers looked at each other. The taller one made a motion with his head, and the two of them dragged the deer the rest of the way to the fence. As Alan watched them, he could hear Todd speaking into the phone and giving directions to the ranch.

As the men came over the fence, Todd laid the cell phone on the pickup seat, put on his sunglasses, and went back to stand by his rifle. Alan got out of the cab and stood by the passenger door as the two men went down into the roadside ditch and came back up.

They were both dark-featured, bearded, with long hair hanging out from beneath their caps. One of them was a stringy fellow, not very tall, and the other was a little huskier. The skinny one had a straight-bladed sheath knife on his belt. Alan recognized both of them, but he didn't know their names. They were roofers he'd seen on jobs here and there as well as in the bars.

"I don't suppose you have permission to hunt here," Todd said. He shook out a cigarette, tapped the filter end on his lighter, put the cigarette in his mouth, and lit it.

The husky one answered. "No, not really. We took a shot at him on the side of the road here, and he jumped the fence, so we had to go after him."

"That doesn't make it a hell of a lot better."

The man shrugged. "Well, that's the way it happened." He looked at his partner. "I guess one of us should tag it."

Todd shot out a cloud of smoke. "I don't know where it'd do you any good." He flicked his thumb on the cigarette filter. "And I'd recommend you not cross that fence again."

The two men looked at each other and back at Todd. Then the smaller one glanced at Alan, as if to say, this is the way you sons of bitches are.

* * * * *

The game warden was all business and curt politeness, with his sunglasses and clipboard, and a holstered pistol high on his right hip. He got Todd's story first, then the road-hunters' story.

"Let's go look at it," he said, then corrected himself. "I mean, let me go look at it. All of you stay here." He laid his clipboard on the hood of Todd's pickup.

The two trespassers sat on the tailgate of their pickup, dangling their legs and smoking, as the game warden walked down into the ditch and up on the other side. He squatted to look at the deer, then stood up and turned around.

"Just one shot?"

The road-hunters both said, "Yeah."

The sunglasses, red shirt, and pistol went down and came back up out of the ditch. The warden looked at the husky man, who had admitted pulling the trigger. "You shot him in the neck. A deer can't jump a fence when he's been neck-shot. You know that. He went down right where he was standing, didn't he?"

The hunter shrugged. "I guess maybe he did."

The game warden picked his clipboard off the hood of the pickup. "I just wanted to get the story straight. It doesn't change anything. You still fired from the road, trespassed, and failed to tag the animal."

The guilty hunter jerked his thumb toward Todd. "He told me not to."

The game warden drew a pen out of his shirt pocket and brought it to bear on the clipboard. "You're the one that pulled the trigger. It's your responsibility. He's not even the landowner." He glanced at Todd and then at the rifle, which was still on the hood. "Are you through with that?"

"Oh, yeah." Todd lifted the rifle, swung it around, and poked it in the gun rack.

The warden turned to the road-hunters. "If you two boys will do me the favor of dragging that deer over here, I'll start writing this up." He looked at Todd and back at them. "You understand, I'll have to put it in the freezer for evidence, in case this goes to trial."

* * * * *

By the time the game warden and the road-hunters left, it was noon. Todd and Alan went back to the ranch to eat lunch in the shade of the elm trees near the house.

Alan had felt a tightness in his stomach for the last hour. He had not enjoyed Todd's show of authority, borrowed as it was. On the other hand, he didn't like the hard look that the hunter gave him. It accused him of being on Todd's side, which he didn't think he was; that, in turn, made him feel like a traitor to the road-hunters, and he wasn't on their side, either. He decided to start a conversation on some other topic. "Where do you think Jay is today?"

"Oh, probably at his house in town."

Alan chewed on his sandwich and nodded. He had thought of how nice it would be to have a place like this in the country. Some of the good feeling went away when he saw how Todd derived a sense of power from being associated with property, but the place itself was still worth appreciating. "Did he buy this as a kind of second place, or weekend getaway, or something?"

"Not really, I don't think. He just saw it at a good price, and my guess is he'll turn it around when he can sell it for what looks like a good deal to him."

"It's a nice place."

Todd reached into his bag of potato chips. "Yeah, but all of these places go broke. The only way to make anything off of 'em is to sell 'em to people from out of state."

Alan nodded. That seemed to be the current trend. People would sell out in a place like Colorado or California and then come here, where their money would go a lot farther. For people like Todd and Jay, it was just property. For the new-comers, it was another chance to hang onto the dream of having land. They had a right to it, he supposed. It was more than he could imagine for himself, for the time being, anyway. He and Sheila needed to get things straightened out so they could get married, move into a better house, and start getting ready for the baby. That was as much as he could think of for now; it was good enough to drive an old pickup and live in a two-bedroom rental. They were just getting their feet on the ground.

Todd looked at his watch. "Those guys took up the rest of the morning. Best part of the day is gone."

"Uh-huh."

"I suppose we could hang around here till late afternoon, or we could just go back into town. Come back and try this some other time."

Alan realized he was being non-committal about the run-in with the road-hunters because he felt it was the exchange for being allowed to hunt on this place. Now he didn't care if he hunted here again. "That might be the best plan," he said.

On the way back into town, Todd said he thought he'd like to go have a cool one and watch the Nebraska game.

Alan said it sounded like a good idea but he had things to catch up on at home. He looked out the pickup window and saw the rangeland stretching away to the west. He thought of the two road-hunters and how their day had turned out, and he thought of how pleased Todd would be to tell the story to Jay.

As he watched the landscape go by, he recalled another job he had been on, a couple of years back. It was a ranch-style house out in the country, on a hill with a good view to the south. The roofing crew had come to put on the shingles, and towards the end of the day he had seen one of the men standing up near the peak of the roof and taking in a view of the countryside. It was a different roofer, not one of these two, but cut from the same sort of cloth. He was tall and lean, with long blond hair and a wispy mustache and chin beard. He stood with his hand resting on his roofer's ax, which hung in his tool belt, and he had a faint smile on his face, as if he were appreciating the piece of life that the homeowners would have. That was how it had seemed to Alan, and now he wondered, again, how much of the good life that fellow, or these two today, would get to have.

Back in town, Todd asked if Alan would like to go out and give it another try in the morning.

Alan said he didn't think so. Sheila had something planned. As he got out of the pickup, he said, "Tell Jay thanks for me. I appreciated the opportunity."

* * * * *

That night at dinner, Alan told Sheila the story about the road-hunters. "I just didn't like it. Here was Todd, all self-righteous about property that wasn't even his, just so he could be in the clique, I guess. And here were these other two guys that I couldn't feel sorry for, but they still made me feel guilty for helping Todd bust 'em." He buttered his bread. "Well, the season lasts two weeks, and I can try to find somewhere else to hunt." He looked at the jelly jar, and he thought of how nice it would be to have some deer meat to go along with what they had put up earlier.

Sheila's dark eyes were soft. "It's too bad it didn't work out. But you can hunt in the National Forest, can't you?"

He shrugged. "I guess so. It's a longer drive, and there's always a ton of hunters." He gave a short, nervous laugh. "But it's better than road-hunting." As he looked at her, he felt calmer; he loved the way her dark hair fell on her shoulders. "I could give it a try, since I have the license and ought to go somewhere. Would you want to go along?"

"Sure. We had a good time when we went in August."

"We'd have to stay overnight, and I'd be out all day, tromping around."

"Oh, that's O.K. I can rest up. And maybe some horses will drop in to pay a visit."

Alan smiled at a memory they had shared several times, about one part of the day they had picked chokecherries. After they had worked for a couple of hours and finally had about five gallons of the small dark fruit, a band of horses came across the open range and stopped to visit. A little black horse went straight to the tailgate, pushed his muzzle down into one of the buckets, and came up with a mouthful.

"That was a nice horse," he said. "It would be fun to see him again." They had talked about how they would like to have a horse some day. It was a thought, at least, that maybe they could, by the time the baby would be old enough to ride. Of course it would cost, like most things would. In the meanwhile it was nice to remember the little black horse that seemed to know, as he and Sheila did, that chokecherries were free.

Memoirs of the Old Scout

I had shot my third gopher of the season—this one like the other two, with my shotgun as he poked his head up out of his burrow—and I was hooking him out with a bent piece of heavy- gauge wire that I keep for that purpose, when it occurred to me that I might write my memoirs, as there might be some people who would be interested to know how a man came to be a killer of animals, how he got into and out of so many important domestic relationships and yet lived most of his life alone.

That's the way the thought came to me on that warm Wednesday afternoon in August as I fished out the dead gopher and carried him to the little dumping ground on the west edge of my place. I shook the wire and dropped the carcass where I have tossed so many mice and magpies and jackrabbits. And, really, those three have been much more of a plague than the gophers. I mention the gophers because of the moment when I first thought about writing my memoirs.

I can see already that I will have to spend some time explaining why it is necessary to kill animals that go to the dump instead of the kitchen. I remember a time when I was called for jury duty in a case in which a man was suing his mother in some long feud over money and property. The man's attorney was talking to the prospective jurors (I hadn't been called to the box), and he asked if there was anybody who was biased against the idea that a man might find it necessary to sue his mother. I didn't get selected for that jury, so I never did find out why such a thing could be necessary, but it does seem like one of those ideas that might be normal to some people but need explanation with others. That's how I see this business about shooting magpies and jackrabbits, and drowning mice, and drawing a bead on a gopher head when it comes pushing up through a soft mound of dirt.

I will try to put all of this in perspective. There was a time when I didn't even kill jackrabbits, back when I used to let myself get paralyzed for the love of a woman, and I would see where the jackrabbits girdled my ash trees and apple trees. But there comes a time when you have to stand up for yourself and for what you think you have at stake, and so the time came for me to fight back.

You might think someone who is called or calls himself the Old Scout would be a greybeard, drooling tobacco juice and smelling of bear grease, and talking like Davy Crockett. My beard is running to grey now, especially since my fated affair with the woman who seems to have stood me up, but I'm not illiterate. I've dipped into a book here and there and have sipped from the fount of knowledge, and there's one saying I keep around. *Il faut manger*. It's French, pronounced "ill foe mawn-jay" if you say it pretty fast, and it means, it is necessary to eat. That explains most of my story. I also take it to mean that in the long run you've got to look out for your own ass, and that covers the rest of my story.

I suppose I didn't look out for myself because I thought it would be bad form to be assertive, what with her being married and all. Waiting for her to make up her mind, I went through a long period of stasis, when I didn't feel I could do much. One might wonder why I waited at all, or why I thought anything was worth waiting for. I had faith that deep down, she believed as I did. She had given me a key chain with a little gold-backed ivory plate attached. On the field of ivory was a pair of quail, a token of how we saw ourselves. I kept it through all the deadlock and beyond. When I looked at it, I did not have to ask or answer the question of why.

Time came and went, but still I did not have the distance that came with time, or the distance that came with distance, to do something about my own paralysis. I thought that someday I would have the perspective to write about it all, but even now, as I begin to write the memoirs, I know that I am focusing on the gophers and the jackrabbits—the parts that I can define and deal with. I hope that some day I can write through the obvious and bring myself to focus on the pretty parts that caused all the pain—for example, the lilacs blooming at the roadside rest where we would meet, the apple blossoms I brought for her on our last lunch, or the cool dusk outside the hotel lobby in Cheyenne.

These memoirs might not end up long enough to be a book, which means there wouldn't be a place for one of those pages where the author thanks all the people who have helped. I didn't get any money from the Rockefellers or the government, and I didn't have any special help from librarians, research assistants, or typists. But if I were to write one of those pages, I would have something to say. It would go like this:

> I would like to thank the people who helped me in my preparation of this work: the cashier at Country General who sold me rifle shells and rat poison, the cashier at Wal-Mart who sold me condoms, and the salesclerk at Zale's who sold me the beautiful jewelry I may never see again.

Then, if these memoirs get long enough, I can move this to the front. Otherwise, I'll leave it right here where I thought of it.

Now, back to *Il faut manger*, or the first part of it. I know that from the time I was a little boy I was interested in food and where it came from. I grew up in a family of butchers, ranchers, farmers, and hunters, and at an early age I knew the smells of rendered lard and scalded chicken feathers. I knew the taste of pheasant even when it went by the name of chicken, and I knew the taste of jackrabbit, which went by no other name because there was no season on it. I knew how hard it was to catch a pig or kill a rat, and how easy it was to squash tomato worms. It all held my interest, and when I first read *Robinson Crusoe*, my strongest impression was how fine it would be to raise my own grapes and goats. As for his living alone, that did not seem strange to me, and as I look back I can see that from the beginning I was suited for a life in which I could store a slaughtered pig in the coolness of a dry lion-claw bathtub and have no one to offend.

When I was old enough to get my own work, I was always content to work in the crops, even though it was hard, sweaty work at low pay. It seemed to be the right thing to do. Later, when I was my own master to the point of being able to rent a place that had a yard or acreage, I felt it my duty to put in a garden. And before I moved to a place where wildlife is plentiful, I also raised rabbits, goats, sheep, hogs, and beef cattle. Instead of golfing or playing tennis, I spent my spare time earning my own food by the sweat of my brow. I felt that as long as I was able to raise or gather my own food, it would be wrong not to.

Il faut manger, and I took the idea into my own hands. When rats got into my livestock feed and rabbit pens, I learned to trap the rodents. For the most part I trapped them as I had done as a boy, but I remember one occasion when I had to get clever. A rat had been leaving turds in the rabbit feeder, and the doe became spooky. I moved her and her nest box to another cage, left feed in the feeder, and set a trap. After a few days of trying one bait and another, I got *monsieur le rat* with bacon grease, and that disgusting episode was closed.

I remember shopping for the traps. I went to a hardware store and described the jaw traps I had in mind. The man in the store took me to a back room and showed me his selection. He explained that he kept them off the main floor because some customers objected to the cruel devices. Naturally, he was in safe company with me, the two of us exchanging a knowing look and turning down the corners of our mouths as we stood in that back room where the traps hung from a nail driven into an unfinished four-by-four.

Now as I think of sending my memoirs out into the world, I realize there are readers who will object to my trapping rats or even shooting them, as I also did. But imagine, gentle reader, that you were such a person who chose to manage your own diet, for reasons of economy, self-sufficiency, and clean victuals. And then you saw a rat where you kept the grain for your goats, or you saw evil rat turds in the clean aluminum feeder where your doe rabbit ate, less than two feet away from the nest box where her pink babies squirmed in their clean bed of wood shavings and fur. You might think, as I did, that the rat was going against the larger plan. Then, still hoping to keep your plan a clean one, you, too, might find yourself looking at shiny new jaw traps, each hanging from its chain with a ring on the end—this ring hanging from a nail driven into an unfinished post in a room where people of the gentlest tendencies do not go.

Once during that era I answered a knock on the door, and I was met by a man who wanted to know who owned the place next door. He said he wanted to photograph the ground squirrels that had such a fine colony in the almond orchard. In the course of the conversation I mentioned that I had gotten quite a bit of practice shooting these ground squirrels, in the almond trees on the place I rented as well as in the orchard across the fence, all of which at one time had been a single orchard. He let me know that he used to hunt with a rifle, then went to a bow, and now hunted with a camera. It was the first time I had heard this evolutionary idea expressed, although I have heard it a few more times in the years since then. I was a brash young man, without a single grey hair yet, and years away from even my first marriage. The photographer presented his point of view in a calm tone, as if to say that I might find such a spiritual growth some day. But here I am a score of years later, my aim much better, wondering if I'll get another gopher before the cold weather sets in.

There was a time, as I suggested earlier, when I think I might have gone soft. I'm not sure. I was so in love with the woman that I took all aspects of life seriously. I was trying to live in harmony with the earth, and I was on the pendulum that I have ridden for years on the subject of shooting coyotes. I got to feeling so reverent about all things that I decided not to kill any coyotes, even when they walked past my house. Furthermore, I turned down an invitation to go stake out a dead cow with a professional guide and coyote hunter, at no charge. I don't know if I was soft in the head then—it might have just been philosophy—but I think I was soft.

I have a general memory of the next several months, in which life was more desolate than ever. I felt as if I lived in a barren landscape that stretched on and on, with motionless windmills and ugly jackrabbits. I would come straight home from work and sit on the couch, where I would gaze out the window to the southwest and watch the sun set. Sometimes I saw deer, or coyotes, or a hawk, and I remembered the springtime when I saw a fox playing with her three cubs on the hillside. Now in the shorter days, the country had gone grey and brown; the shadows lengthened early and the air chilled. Sometimes an owl came to the telephone pole and hooted to another owl. The cool air also carried the sound of the pheasant roosters as they drummed their wings and crowed their short, unbroken call. At dusk the wild geese flew over, swishing their wings as they wheezed and whistled and honked on their way north. There was a lot to see and appreciate, but I felt closed up. All I could sense was the bleakness. When the sun started moving north again, my energy was still at a low ebb, and I had to push myself to go out and take walks.

On one excursion, I came out of my torpor long enough to notice a five-gallon can tipped on its side. It was an old, rusty, bullet-riddled fuel can with a three-inch opening that at one time took a threaded cap. In place of the cap was the neck of a skunk, with the body of the animal draped down and resting on the ground. It looked as if the skunk had wiggled his head into the opening and then couldn't get it out. It was typical negligence in farm country, I thought, to leave debris lying around to do unexpected harm. Then it occurred to me that the skunk had decided to put his head into the hole and that after getting stuck, he hadn't thought much about whose fault it was.

On another walk, farther from my house and the potential ring of the phone, I walked along the edge of a cornfield and saw a goose-hunting pit. It consisted of a large wooden box, maybe six feet by six feet by ten feet, sunk into the ground. It had a loose plywood cover with hatch doors that slid aside. I had seen it the year before. As the cover was not nailed down, I had taken careful steps to get a peek. I scooted one of the hatch doors aside, and I was embarrassed by what I saw. Someone had left newspapers, styrofoam coffee cups, and half a package of sweet rolls on the wooden table. A folded newspaper lay on the seat of the one wooden chair I saw. I closed the hatch, feeling as if I had looked in through someone's window and had seen the bed unmade.

Now, a year later, the plywood top had fallen into the pit and had just a corner sticking up. With even more care than before, I walked up to the edge and peered over. Now I saw the remains of a dead cow, long dead and dried out, with bones showing at the neck and ribs. It was contorted, with its head propped against the table, its feet upward, and its body slumped on the floor. I backed away.

Again, I thought about carelessness—this time of the farmers and hunters both. Then I thought about the cow, thrashing helplessly and not thinking about whose fault it was but only trying to make sense of a sky framed by the wooden sides of the pit. It reminded me of the skunk, trying to make sense of the inside of a fuel can with a little bit of sunlight coming in through the bullet holes. In the end, I thought, those animals were like the rest of us, only worse off; they were in a bad spot and didn't know what to do about it.

So maybe I wasn't soft—just helpless. I know I was woozy a year later, when I was still waiting for the same woman to call me. It was that time of year when we were coming out of the deep freeze of winter but I hadn't started working the garden plot yet. It was late afternoon and I was sitting, powerless and morose, on my sofa. I could see the garden area. Then I saw five jackrabbits come onto my garden plot and begin to joust around.

I date this as a low point in my life. I was so run into the ground by despair and lost hope that I did not even shoot at the jackrabbits. I told myself we could all live together. Yes, that's what I did, my spirit was so low.

Then I saw where they had stripped the bark from my young ash trees and where they had chewed a wide band around the base of my small apple trees. I became indignant. You might say my self-respect rose from the floor. I began shooting jackrabbits. I thought, if I am going to work my ass off to try to grow shade trees and fruit in this rugged climate, I am not going to lie back and watch it all go to hell.

And really, it's the same with the magpies. They would eat my whole crop of strawberries and then all my chokecherries if I didn't protest with my shotgun. Sometimes I drive home along the lane to my house and see them rise, twenty or thirty in a flock, from the deer bones I have thrown to my dogs. If I didn't kill a few, the flock would be twice that size and twice that impudent.

It just took some doing—it took the nerve to stand up to myself and say, I'm taking some of my life into my own hands.

Maybe I am wrong. Maybe there would be the same number of both of these pests whether I shot them or not. But at least this way, I give myself the feeling that I am doing something to look out for my own interests. I also give myself the feeling that I'm not letting the sons of bitches walk all over me. That seems important.

I haven't kept count of how many jackrabbits I have killed, but I know I have gotten occasional satisfaction by making a good shot. I remember one that I drilled dead center, at about fifty yards. He leapt straight up in the air and turned, showing his white underside, and landed dead, facing in the opposite direction. Later that day, when I got home from work, I saw that the scavengers had pecked out his exposed eyeball and had made quite an entry in his abdomen. On later occasions I would see the same pattern of plundering. One remains objective at times like this, being satisfied with protecting one's interests and in doing it with some competency.

I recall an instance, in the evening after a rain shower, when I made another good shot. Again the white-grey underbelly flashed as the animal jumped and flopped. I took the occasion to go observe the dark hocks, the powdery black rump and tail, the black tips on the ears. By the time I had put the rifle away, a magpie had landed; I left him undisturbed. The next morning, I saw a small hawk, not much larger than a magpie, with white feathered legs, standing on the jackrabbit. He would dip his curved beak down into the carcass and pull up strands of flesh and bloody gut. With each mouthful he would look to right and left, then ingest, and then take another dip. The magpies would light nearby and hop around, keeping their distance and waiting their turn.

I doubt that the magpies or the hawk gave much thought to the events that led to this opportunity, and I am sure they could not have worried about how fairly I did my work, but I have tried to maintain my own sense of fairness. I recall another occasion, at day's end, when I caught sight of what I thought was a jackrabbit. The flamboyant tones of sunset reflected off of a salmon-colored object that stuck out from the dry cheat grass. The object looked like the head and ears of my adversary. I went for the rifle and, not wanting to shoot at a ball of fur, walked toward it. When the object expanded into a running jackrabbit with black tail, white rump, and black-tipped ears, zigging and zagging, I brought up the rifle and made a good shot. I remember this incident because of my restraint in waiting until he ran his colors aloft.

I believe I have almost always tried to play fair. I can think of once when it seemed as if I didn't, but even at that it's hard to say, as fairness is such a relative matter.

I was driving along the dirt road that leads from my place to the paved road. I had the headlights on, and I had a bit of optimism flowing in my veins; I had my checkbook in my left boot, two condoms in my right boot, and a black hat stuck on my head. Feeling like a happy cowboy and thinking to put solitude behind me for a few hours, I was headed toward the Broncho Bar.

A jackrabbit sprang up out of the dead weeds of winter and took out straight ahead of me. A year or so earlier, I might not have done anything, but by now I had committed myself to a vendetta against jackrabbits, so I stepped on the gas. My old pickup gave a lurch and then steadied out, accelerating to thirty miles an hour, with the headlight beams on the animal's black tail and then on the black tips of his ears and then nothing. Hearing no *thump*, I guessed he had turned aside just as I got up on him and couldn't see him anymore. I slowed down as I approached the paved road, and lo! there emerged *monsieur le lièvre*, black eartips straightening up as he pulled back out ahead of me in the headlights.

I felt ashamed, as well I should. No one could expect me to go out and chase a rabbit on foot, or to limit myself to flinging stones and sticks, but in a relative scale of fairness, I felt I had cheated by using a Chevy V-8. I was glad the fellow got away, perhaps to come back and give me a chance on terms that would seem fairer—to me, at least.

I remember reading, not long after that, an argument in favor of hunting coyotes with greyhounds. According to the author, using dogs to run down the coyote and tear it apart is more sporting than using a rifle to reach across the distance or a four-wheeled motorcycle to close up the distance. Showing disdain for varmint guns and four-wheelers, the author wrote, "To the true coyote hunter, there is no sport in this." It struck me as being spoken with a genuine sense of fairness— relative, like my own, but principled.

So I count that moment of weakness, the moment when I yielded to the temptation to use the machine, as a bad one. It wasn't fair, even if in someone else's system there would be true sport in it.

After all, one remembers that the rules of engagement are relative. The true coyote hunter looks down on guns and motorcycles, but he hauls around his coyote dogs in a pickup. The reverent bow-hunter or photographer drives to the area where he plans to hunt.

With jackrabbits, I draw the line at using a .22 magnum. It has seemed fair to me. I remember one fellow I got, a wily one, and I believe I did it with honor. He had long ears, like broomsticks, and for all I know the length may have helped him hear better. I saw him one night in the moonlight, from the kitchen, but he heard me open the window. On a couple of other occasions, also, he evaded me. Some jackrabbits have a way of running in which they keep the head low and forward, like a buck antelope, and when they go between two clumps of sagebrush, they duck the head like a deer will duck his antlers. That was the way this one ran, like a crafty buck. Then one afternoon, in broad daylight, after I rolled into the yard, vaunted at any mice that might have been in the live trap, and walked into the house, I saw my long-eared foe in the garden. With some guile I eased the window open, snicked a shell into place, and—yes—I got him. Then, as I have often done, I went for the pitchfork, carried the carcass out to the heap and dumped it, and then cleaned off the tines of the fork by running them back and forth through the granulated mound of an anthill.

No doubt there are some who will think that what I did was not fair—perhaps they would draw the line at cranking open the window, or even at using the rifle. Very well, I say. Tell me I have cheated. In my defense I can say there's no sweeter cheater than my .22 mag, and I have to say that even that remark is a satisfying exercise in control. Of course it is based on my having decided to take a course of action to begin with.

Shooting jackrabbits was not the only way I built up my fortitude, but it is a good outward indication of what was going on inside. I was getting better. Here I had been despondent, lying around in despair because the phone wouldn't ring, and then little by little, thanks to my assertion, I found myself going out on the weekends (as noted above), traveling away from the phone for more than a day at a time, and more or less living my life. It happened over a period of several months, and I can't say that I got over my feelings for the woman I was waiting to hear from. But things did begin to change and I did begin to take initiative, and I relate it to that decisive period when I got out the rifle.

Now I will digress and tell about a form of passivity I went through, not unlike the inaction I had fallen into before I began shooting jackrabbits. In that same year, I photographed quite a few flowers. My idea was that since my intended could not be with me, I would save all the pictures of the daffodils, the tulips, the lilacs, the poppies, the snapdragons, the gladiolas, and so on. I would save the pictures, squirrel them away in an album, and then bring them out to share when we were together. It helped me bide my time, and since it was a good gardening season, I ended up with several nice photographs (which she never saw).

So I went through a phase of hunting with a camera after all, but in spite of it I began my recovery as I described above, when I began to shoot jackrabbits. It was during this time that I saw a mound of dirt in the tulip beds. With no more guile than I would use to kill a jackrabbit, I tried to drygulch the gopher by opening the kitchen window. He heard me, I didn't get a shot, and he went back under. The hills multiplied, and after some time they began to show up on the other side of the yard, beyond the lilac bushes. One day I looked out the living room window and saw dirt coming out of the ground, so I crept outside and made a careful sneak with the lilac bushes as my cover, and my efforts were rewarded by the sight of a gopher head poking up.

That was the first gopher I got with a shotgun, and I felt victorious. I disposed of the carcass, tamped dirt down the holes, and went about my projects. But I was yet to learn that gophers would not take that easy a dismissal. Within a week or so I saw new mounds in the tulip beds, but I could not see the work in progress. Finally I resorted to putting rat poison down the hole, and I think I might have gotten some results. The fresh mounds ceased to appear within a month or so, and then I didn't think much about gophers for quite a while.

Over a couple of years I noticed that I had fewer tulips and daffodils, and I wondered why. It didn't occur to me until much later that the hidden enemy had done his damage quite a while back and that it took me a long time to see how he had worked against my efforts.

By now I was into the present season (from which I write) and had pretty well given up on the woman who seemed to have strung me out, when a new surge of gopher activity came on. Perhaps the earlier gophers had blazed the trail, and this was the wave of settlers. I saw mounds come up all over—in the flower beds, in the lawn, across the driveway in the marigold strip. Then came the time of reckoning referred to earlier, when in a space of a couple of weeks I killed three gophers, lifting each one halfway out of its hole with a blast of the twelve-gauge. It was after that remarkable series of ambushes that I decided to write these memoirs.

Time passed as I wrote, laid down my pen, took it up again, and made my way through the stories about the rats and the ground squirrels and the jackrabbits. Then I had to quit writing, because a new gopher moved in. I knew it was a new gopher because I had killed the others, but I couldn't resist the sense that it had been there all the time and was just letting itself be seen again. Now I felt I couldn't write my memoirs in a decisive way until I had some resolution. I had to have some control, some dominance, over my problem. How, thought I, could I write about being an Old Scout if such an aspect of it was buried beyond my reach, working against me as I wrote? At the very least, I felt I had to kill this latest gopher, too.

Fall was coming on, and I noticed new gopher mounds out in the pastures and down in the fruit orchard. I imagined this fellow was getting dug in for the winter. I didn't like the idea, because I had ordered about a hundred and fifty tulip bulbs, and I needed to plant them before the ground froze. So I planted the bulbs and kept an eye out for my nemesis.

On the last day of September, I spent a day working on end-of-the-season chores, and I dug out part of a new tunnel. After quite a bit of waiting and discreet peeking, I saw a brown furry streak pushing dirt across the hole I had dug out. I timed my shot and fired, and to my great surprise I missed.

For the next two months, the gopher had me in a state of anxiety. I dug out the tunnels here and there, but never to any avail. I saw new mounds appear, sometimes two or three a day, but I could not see the gopher. I thought he knew me too well, heard me coming and going, and knew not to show his head when I was around.

Then he moved back toward the house and into the tulip beds. More mounds appeared, and I had the helpless feeling that I could do nothing about this industry. I would peek out in the morning, see the dark new soil with frost on it, and see where my antagonist had made another move against me. I began to think I was going to have to order a gopher trap—a gruesome gadget, and not really in the spirit of things as I had been trying to manage them.

Finally, on one Sunday morning at about 8:00, I saw a new mound of dark soil. I had not seen it half an hour earlier, so I imagined my little foe was at work. I watched, and then I saw the duller grey-tan head of the gopher push up and through the soft, loose dirt. With all my cunning I fetched the shotgun, made ready, got my timing as the head pushed up and paused, and made a successful shot. I was a happy boy as I went to fetch my wire, and as I hooked the gopher and pulled it up out of its burrow, I saw it was a fat one. I thought it should be, with all the tulips I had planted.

Now we are into winter, and no new gophers have shown evidence of moving in. I have knocked down and raked out all the mounds, and I feel I have the upper hand for the time being.

That has given me the sense of resolution I needed to finish this first chapter, which has been a good thing for me to write, as it has given me a small sense of control.

None of this is as easy as it might seem. I remember reading a magazine article about a celebrity who had gotten into a very ill-advised love affair. The reporter made the sage comment that although we may not be able to choose who it is we fall in love with, we can choose what to do about it. At the same time that I saw some truth in the comment, I wondered if the writer had ever taken the big plunge, had ever risked so much for the sake of what seemed so real. I thought that a person who had ever fallen in love good and deep would not make such an easy generality about what people can choose.

All the same, I suppose there are ways by which we can try to gain some measure of control over what we have done, if not over what we will do. One way is to go to the gun closet. Another way is to dwell on images, like the key chain she gave me. Another way is to use words. I suppose my best effort in doing something about the problem has been to work on these memoirs. There was a long time when I couldn't put any of it into words, when I just looked at the key chain and ivory, and even now I have found it easier to focus on what I did or didn't do rather than on why we fell in love in the first place.

I remember reading, during the middle of the dreariest siege, a short novel called *My Mortal Enemy*. The mortal enemy in that work was love—sublunary love, the type that takes the form of lilacs, apple blossoms, and dusky evenings when one person gives another a key chain. In the novel, the mortal enemy kept the main character from fulfilling her own potential. But I have arrived at a different conclusion than the one I might have derived out of the book: I believe the mortal enemy is worth it, even if it kicks your ass.

And if I have learned one other thing out of all of this, it is that things are never really over. I know better than to think I have done with the jackrabbits and gophers any more than I am finished writing my memoirs or even having reasons to write them. If I hope to see tulips and eat apples, I had better keep a shotgun and rifle handy, and not trade them in for a camera. And if I hope to share the flowers and fruit with someone else, it is just as well that I flinch sometimes when I see the red light that tells me I have a phone message. Sooth to say, I hope to hear from her again, if only to find out what it all meant. And if I do hear from her, or see her, I need to do a better job of looking out for my own well-being. As the old scouts used to say, my hair might be grey but I aim to keep it.

One Cold Night at the Quadrille

Snow was beginning to pile up around the gas pumps and in the parking lot. The one car in front of the restaurant—a tan Buick with Sheridan County plates—had dirty ice hanging along the undersides, and the snow was still melting on the windshield and back window. Sam imagined the car had pulled in in the last little while, just as he was doing, in obedience to the long arm with the "Road Closed" sign that lay across the southbound lane of the highway right outside the restaurant. Depending on when the highway further north got closed, there might be a few more travelers obliged to stop at the Quadrille.

Sam parked on the right side of the Buick and shut off the engine. "Well, I guess we'll be here for a while," he said.

T.J. nodded. "There are worse places."

Sam pursed his lips. "I can think of a few." He glanced at the rifles hanging in the rack. "I suppose we should lock up."

T.J. took his sheath knife off the dashboard and set it on the seat next to a box of .30-06 shells. "Probably not a bad idea."

Inside the Quadrille, Sam renewed his familiarity with the place. The front door led into the center of the dining area, which consisted of half a dozen tables and a counter with stools. Behind the counter, a wall with a pass-through window divided the service area from the kitchen. To the right of the restaurant, a door led into the bar. As Sam recalled, a person had to go through the bar to get to the rest rooms.

A waitress probably in her late twenties, with dark hair pulled back and held with a barrette, stood in back of the counter, smiling. As Sam waited for T.J. to close the door, he felt the cold air following them into the warm restaurant. He heard the door close, and then the waitress asked if they would like to be seated.

T.J.'s voice came up at Sam's right. "Is the bar open?"

The waitress nodded. "Yes, it is. I'll tell Morris." She turned and went into the kitchen.

Sam noticed an older couple, the man wearing a tan short-brimmed hat, sitting at a table to his left. They had nothing more than coffee in front of them. That was good. No one should feel an obligation to order a meal right away, as there had been no choice about where to stop. They would all end up ordering meals anyway. He glanced at the dark interior beyond the open doorway, then gave a tiny frown as he turned to T.J. "I guess we wait, huh?"

T.J. pushed out his lower lip and nodded.

A man who looked as if he could be Morris came out of the kitchen, walked around in front of the counter, smiled, and led the way to the bar. As he flicked a light switch inside the doorway, a hanging Budweiser sign lit up and shed light over a pool table. The man turned to his left and flipped another switch, and an array of beer and liquor signs brightened the area behind the bar.

Sam and T.J. took stools at the bar, which ran parallel with the wall blocking off the kitchen. From where he sat, Sam could see into the dining area, and with a slight turn to the left he could see through a window that looked west onto the parking lot.

"Well, what'll it be, boys?"

"Bottle of Coors," said T.J. "Are you Morris?"

"Sure am. And you?"

"I'm T.J., and this is Sam."

Morris nodded. "My pleasure." He looked at Sam. "And you, another Coors?"

"Sure." As Morris moved away, Sam turned on his stool and looked around. The bar and pool room must have been added on to the restaurant. The dining room had a wood floor, while this part had a painted cement floor. In the back of the room, to the south, a small window looked out upon drab grassland, blurred now in driving snow.

Morris set the two beers in front of his patrons. "Been hunting?"

"Uh-huh." Sam took out a five-dollar bill and set it on the bar.

"Weather shut you down?"

"Nope. Not really. We got our two antelope this morning, and we were headed back when we saw the road was closed."

"Oh, uh-huh." Morris stood there, in no apparent hurry to pick up the money. "Goin' south?"

Sam lifted his beer. "Yeah. We're from Linton."

Morris nodded and moved away with the money.

A movement at Sam's left caught his eye. He looked out the window and saw a maroon-colored Oldsmobile settling to a stop. The county number on the license plate was twenty-one.

"Looks like someone else just pulled in," he said, as Morris laid the change on the bar.

"Uh-huh. Must be from Newcastle."

Sam looked at Morris. The man had a full head of hair, greying and combed back; his brown were eyes set in a middle-aged face that had begun to fill out. He was clean-shaven, with light-colored sideburns that came halfway down the ear.

Sam looked out the window and saw two grey-haired ladies getting out of the car. Then he turned back to the bar at the sound of T.J.'s voice.

"What's 'Quadrille' mean?"

Morris reached into the pocket of his brown flannel shirt and pulled out a pack of Marlboros. "Two things." He shook out a cigarette and lit it with a lighter he picked up from below the bar. After he blew away a cloud of smoke he said, "It could be a four-handed game of cards, or it could be a square dance."

Sam had the impression that Morris had answered the question a hundred times but hadn't gotten tired of it.

"That makes sense," said T.J. "Quadrilateral. Square. Did they have square dances at this place at one time?"

Morris shrugged. "I don't know. I've had the place for four years, but the name goes way back." He set his cigarette in the ashtray and turned away to go to the restaurant.

Sam watched the front door as it opened. The two ladies, both of them wearing glasses, stepped inside. Sam looked at T.J. “This place might start filling up.”

T.J. gave a backward wave with his left hand. “As long as he doesn’t run out of beer.”

“So far, the others don’t look like much of a threat in that way.”

T.J. was quiet for a moment and then said, “You learn something every day.”

“Uh-huh. About what?”

“Well, like the name of this place. I mean, I’d been here before and all that, but I never knew what it meant. I thought it had something to do with squares, but I didn’t know, and I never took the trouble to ask, much less look it up.”

“Same here.”

“But you know, it would be a good word to describe a month like this one, that begins on a Sunday.”

“Oh, uh-huh.”

“Sure.” T.J. pointed at a calendar on the wall behind the bar. October started with a red Sunday. “When you see it on the calendar, the first four weeks of it, anyway, are as square as can be. And a February that starts on a Sunday would be perfectly square.”

“Yeah.” Sam could picture it, just like October but without the last three days.

“And except on a leap year, February and March always look the same for the first four weeks.”

“Uh-huh.”

"And as far as that's concerned, April and July are always the same, for the first thirty days, just like September and December are."

"Is that right?" Sam didn't mind humoring T.J. when he was showing off what he knew.

"Sure is. Look on the calendar for any year. I checked it out on the perpetual calendar. If April has a Friday the thirteenth, then July does. If September does, December does."

"Hmm." Sam recalled a couple of comments T.J. made the day before, on their drive up, about Friday the thirteenth. If he had any superstitions, they had gone away when the two of them got settled into the barn at the Castlemon Ranch. A pair of T-bones in a skillet on the Coleman stove, plus a bottle of Jim Beam, did a pretty good job of pushing away the rest of the world. And then this morning, when they went out into the teeth of the storm that was moving in, it was all seriousness—cloud and wind and snow, sagebrush, grass, and antelope, then dark blood on the pale grass, steam from the carcasses, and cold water to wash the blood from their hands. Now in the warm comfort of a barroom, maybe T.J. was thinking again about bad luck. Or maybe he was just talking up a clever idea, which he liked to do.

"Don't you think so?"

"Think what?"

"That it would be a good word to describe a month that starts on a Sunday."

Sam shrugged. "I guess so. I don't know if you could get it into the dictionary."

"Well, it's a start. Every new word has to start somewhere. I mean, even a bogus word like 'groovy'—how do you think it got started? Probably with one person, and then it spread out, and then the next thing you knew, every mush-head in the country was using it."

Sam laughed. "You want the mush-heads to use your word?"

"Not necessarily. I just think it's a good word."

"You could ask Morris."

T.J. tipped his head. "Maybe not right away. He might think we were making fun of his place."

Sam made a motion as if he was zipping his lips closed. Then a movement outside the west window made him look at the parking lot. A two-toned Suburban, blue and grey, pulled in next to the maroon Oldsmobile. Sam did not recognize the vehicle even though it had county seven plates.

"More company?" T.J. asked.

"Looks like it." Two men in orange caps and camouflage jackets got out of the front. "I don't know if I recognize them, but they've got the same plates as we do."

T.J.'s voice didn't have much fun in it now. "I think I know who they are."

Sam paused as two more men got out of the back seat of the Suburban. "I've seen a couple of them around, I think."

"Yeah, I have, too. They'll be a lot of fun to get snowed in with."

Sam looked at T.J. "Not friends, I take it?"

T.J. shook his head. "Not by a stretch." Then he smiled. "I don't think there'll be any trouble, though."

* * * * *

The four men took a table in the dining area, not far from the doorway that led into the bar. Sam had a sense of who they were—business men of sorts, all of them in their late thirties or so, maybe a few years older than Sam and T.J. They were the smug type, sure of themselves and likely to keep their distance from wage-working beer drinkers.

T.J. went to the juke box, fed in four quarters that clanked into the machine, and began punching song numbers. Sam picked his two quarters off the bar and walked to the other end of the pool table. As he got closer to the juke box, he could see it was an old one—not the new kind that had rows of CD's and took dollar bills, but the old kind that had numbers like A8, J9, and so forth, and swallowed quarters in the way he had just heard.

Sam put two quarters in the coin tray of the pool table and pushed the plunger; with a clunk the balls dropped into the chute and then rolled down to the end of the table. As he looked up and around, he saw that the other four men had settled into a game of cards and that Morris was pouring four mixed drinks at the bar. The juke box was blaring "Squaws Along the Yukon" when T.J., beer in hand, sauntered over to Sam's end of the pool table.

"You know all four of them?" Sam asked as he set the rack up onto the table.

"Uh-huh. Wheeler-dealers. Or think they are."

"That guy with his back to the door, who is he? I know I've seen him." Sam was crouched now and was lifting the pool balls, two with each hand, up onto the table and into the rack.

"That's Keith Arnett. He's got the insurance agency. And the one on his left, that you can barely see, is Dale Burroughs."

"He does real estate, right?" Sam arranged the balls in alternating order of solid/stripe, solid/stripe.

"Uh-huh. They're natural buddies."

"And the one lookin' at us?"

"That's Stan Cundall. Building contractor."

"Seems like he's given us a couple of looks so far."

"Probably has." T.J. had picked a cue stick off the wall and was sighting along its length.

Sam lifted the rack from the table and set it back into its slot. "And the one with his back to the counter?"

"That's Craig Dickinson. He's got the Wagon Wheel steak house."

"Oh, uh-huh. Now I place him." Sam turned to the wall to get himself a cue stick. "You want to break?"

T.J. nodded, went to the bar to set his beer there, and leaned down to break the rack. "Straight eight?"

"Uh-huh."

Morris came back in and stood behind the bar, so Sam and T.J. gravitated to their stools whenever they weren't taking a shot. Morris made a comment about the other hunters also being from Linton, and from the short answers he got in response, he seemed to get the idea that they weren't all brothers of the same cloth. After he took the next round of highballs and gin-and-tonics to the card players, he came back to the bar and lit a cigarette.

"Well, I talked to my wife in the kitchen, and she heard on the radio that the road is closed south from Newcastle, and both south and north from Mule Creek Junction. So unless someone wants to take a gravel road out through the cow country, I don't think anyone is goin' anywhere till tomorrow morning."

Sam looked at him and said, "So there's ten of us here that you've got on your hands."

Morris smiled as he motioned with his head toward the dining room. "That's what they said, too."

T.J. set his empty Coors bottle on the bar. "Too bad you don't have a hotel."

Morris laughed. "It seems like I've got somethin', one way or the other. But we've managed before."

Sam finished his beer and set the empty next to T.J.'s, then nodded for Morris to set up two Coors while he was at it. "Have you got a plan, then?"

"Oh, we'll wait a little while, till everyone gets used to the idea. Then we'll see who-all wants to sleep in the trailer houses and who wants to sleep here in the restaurant."

Sam gave a short laugh. "Well, I guess we've got all day and night to talk about it. No hurry."

Morris laughed again as he set out the two beers. "None at all. Just drink up."

* * * * *

And so they did. Sam and T.J. each got a couple of dollars' worth of change and set it on the rail of the pool table. They drank their second beer and then a third, all the while listening to the juke box and taking their shots at pool. Nothing moved in a hurry. The quartet playing cards inside the restaurant did not come in to challenge the pool table, and with the exception of an occasional person passing through to use the rest room, the bar crowd stayed the same.

The juke box had a number of old-time honky-tonk songs, which Morris said came from "back when 'E.T.' meant Ernest Tubb." T.J. played a few of them over and over again, especially "Squaws Along the Yukon." After it had played a few times, and with the help of the beer, Sam liked the song well enough to join in with Morris and T.J.

She makes her underwear
From the hide of a grizzly bear
And bathes in ice-cold water every day.
Her skin I love to touch,
But I sure can't touch it much,
Because her fur-lined parka's in the way.

T.J. danced, rocking from one foot to the other, tossing the slender end of his cue stick back and forth from one hand to another as the thick end rested on the floor between his feet. Morris moved his head from one side to the other as he sang along. Sam held up his beer bottle and waved it back and forth.

Oo-ga, oo-ga, moosh-gah,
Which means that I love you,
If you will be my baby,
I'll oo-ga, oo-ga, moosh-gah you.
As I take her hand in mine
And put her on my knee,
The squaws along the Yukon
Are good enough for me.

The wind blew and the snow came down at a slant, piling up on the windshields of the vehicles parked outside. The rest of the world, including bills and work and Monday morning, was all far away. The Quadrille was like Castlemon's barn, except that here they had a juke box, a pool table, and cold beer—plus a few people in the next room, which Sam had been doing pretty well at ignoring.

Morris brought in a dish of crackers and two bowls of chili beans, which he said were on the house. Sam and T.J. let the pool table sit as it was, with half the game yet to play, and they dug into the chili.

"You don't see many of these anymore."

Sam looked up and saw Morris holding between thumb and forefinger a coin that had a red splotch on it. "What is it?"

"A red quarter."

"Did someone paint it?"

"It's the way they used to do it. They usually did it with fingernail polish."

T.J. paused with his spoon on the edge of the bowl. “What did they do that for?”

Morris took on his air of the fellow who liked to know the answer. “In a place like this, the owner or manager or whoever would keep a bunch of ’em in a cup, to get people to play the jukebox. If the bartender or barmaid lost rollin’ the dice, or if they wanted to play a few songs just to liven things up, they’d use the red quarters. Then when the guy came to empty the jukebox, he’d give all the red quarters back to the bar owner.”

“Is that right?” said T.J. “Sort of like primin’ the pump.”

“Uh-huh. And the owners always complained that the red quarters showed up everywhere—in the cash register, in the cigarette machine, in the candy machine.”

“Well, I’ll be damned.” T.J. went back to eating his chili.

“They don’t do it as much as they used to. For one thing, they don’t shake for the music as much in this part of the country. Fact is, you don’t really see dice in the bars here as much as you do in some places.”

Sam shrugged. “Never really thought about it.”

Morris lit a cigarette. “It’s what I’ve noticed. They can play pitch or gin rummy till hell won’t have it, and for quite a little money, but they won’t play poker or roll dice, where they’d have to have the money out in plain view.”

Sam shook his head. “I guess it’s what you’re used to.”

“Uh-huh.”

Morris smoked his cigarette while the other two ate. When they finished, he took their bowls to the kitchen and brought back another serving. He said the people in the other room had all made their phone calls. The old couple from Sheridan and the two ladies from Newcastle had used the restaurant phone, and the other four had used the insurance agent's cell phone. Morris explained that he and his wife, Marilyn, who was the cook, lived in one of the trailer houses, and the waitress, whose name was Jackie, lived in the other trailer with Scott, the dishwasher. The couple from Sheridan, the Andersons, had agreed to stay in Morris and Marilyn's trailer, and the ladies from Newcastle, Shirley and Dorothy, had said they weren't afraid to sleep in the other trailer.

Morris asked if the boys wanted to make any phone calls. Sam said no, he was divorced and didn't have anyone to call, and no one expected them back until Sunday anyway. Morris looked at T.J., who shook his head.

Morris said he didn't know what they thought about sleeping arrangements. Sam said he didn't care where he slept that night. They had their sleeping bags, and if they could sleep in a barn, they could sleep in a bar.

T.J. said he didn't care either.

Morris said that was good. They could sleep in here if they wanted, and the other gentlemen could sleep on the floor of the restaurant. They didn't have sleeping bags, but he thought he could dig up enough bedding for everyone.

Sam and T.J. called for another round, and when Morris set it up, Sam noticed the clock. It was only 4:30 in the afternoon.

They went back to shooting pool and feeding the juke box. The good-time feeling started to flow again. Sam began to take a liking to another song, "Pick Me Up On Your Way

Down." Now that it had played a few times, he could sing a couple of the lines he had learned.

And you've never once looked back
At your home across the track.

T.J. was singing, too. He seemed to know all the songs, all the old beer-drinking, shit-kicking songs. He sang a verse that Sam hadn't learned yet.

They have changed your attitude,
Made you haughty and so rude—

Then when the refrain came around a second time, Sam was able to join in.

Pick me up on your way down,
When you're blue and all alone—
When their glamor starts to bore you,
Come on back where you belong.

Sam looked at Morris, who was singing along as well. The man had a fondness for these old songs. They would be part of a world he held dear—a world of red quarters, leather dice cups, and brave cheer.

Morris came to the south end of the pool table and stood by the window. "There's a couple now," he said. "That's what you need."

Sam looked out and saw two antelope, a buck and a doe, moving at an angle away from the highway, not two hundred yards from the window. They had their white rumps to the wind, and their tan-and-white bodies looked pale in the white world outside. After a few beers and a feed of beans in a warm barroom, Sam was glad not to be out in the storm. "We've used up our permits," he said.

Morris nodded. "Those other four guys say they don't have any antelope licenses. Just deer." He was chewing on a toothpick. "Too bad. I'd cook some up just for the hell of it."

"Hell," T.J. said. "We've got meat chillin' in the back of the pickup. If you want, I'll go cut off enough so everyone can have a steak."

Morris's face took on a broad smile. "That sounds like fun."

T.J. gave him a steady look. "That won't cut into any of your business, will it?"

Morris shook his head. "Nah. I'm gonna sell plenty of food and drinks anyway, and I feel kinda funny as it is, with people stuck here without much choice of where they get their meal."

"Well, could be they don't all care for wild meat. If you let me know how many want a steak, I'll go cut off a hunk."

Morris went into the restaurant and came back in a little while. "We don't have that many takers," he said. "All these other folks said they'd just as soon order off the menu, and none of the kitchen help seemed much interested, so it'd just be you two and me. It's probably not worth the trouble. But

I'll tell you, if they don't open that road up tomorrow, we'll think on it again."

"Good enough," said T.J. "It's not goin' anywhere."

The boys went back to their pool game. A little while later, Sam noticed the waitress taking orders from the customers in the restaurant. Her name was Jackie, as he recalled. She stood at profile, talking to the couple from Sheridan. She wasn't too bad-looking, but there was something Morris had said about her and the dishwasher living in the same trailer. What the hell, he thought, and he let his gaze drift. As he did so, he caught a dirty look from one of the men playing cards. It was the one facing him, the building contractor named Cundall. Well, if he was jealous, or if he had his own fantasy about sleeping with the waitress, that was his problem. Sam turned and looked at the pool table, where T.J. was banking the six-ball into the side pocket. When he looked again, Jackie was serving hamburgers and French fries to the table of four men.

Sam and T.J. played out the game, and Sam lost. He had used up all of his pool table quarters, so he went to the bar. With beer at a dollar-seventy-five a bottle, he got back a dollar bill and two quarters each time he bought a round, so he had a small stack of coins in front of his stool. As he picked two quarters off the bar, he recalled an incident from several years back.

It was in a small town in Nevada, where he was stuck overnight. He found a bar that seemed about right for his means, and he settled in for a few drinks. Beer was a dollar-twenty-five a bottle, so his stack of quarters went up and down, and every once in a while he could drink one beer out of his change. After he paid for his seventh beer, he had five quarters on the bar and expected to come out even. Meanwhile, he had noticed the man on the stool to his right, a young sport in his mid-twenties, who wore a felt cowboy hat with a bandana hatband and a goose feather in it. He was a good-looking fellow, with dark hair and mustache, but with a low-class look to him nevertheless. He was trying to sidle up to a young woman who was complaining about what a jerk her husband was. When any of the other regulars would come up and ask the fellow how he was doing, he would go on about how crummy it was to be out of work, how the contractors brought in help from out of town, what a sonofabitch so-and-so was to get a job with thus-and-such a company, and so on. Eventually, after nursing a beer for a long time, the guy asked for one on credit, which he got. Sam figured he was hanging on in the bar to see if he could get somewhere with the woman.

When Sam was in the middle of the seventh beer, he got up to go to the can. He had the habit of not going to the rest room if he was done with a beer, because someone could come along and take his stool—or, something that might make the difference between drinking another beer or not, the bartender could take his change, thinking it was a tip. So, with five quarters on the bar, he slid off his stool and found the men's room by the back door. When he got back, his beer was still there, but the quarters were gone. The fellow with the bandana hatband seemed surprised to see him again, and with a quarter-turn of his stool he turned to the woman and began speaking in a louder voice about how he was thinking of living in his tent for a while. Then he turned his stool so that he had his back to the bar. Still speaking to the woman and calling out a comment now and then to one of the guys at the pool table, he sat like that for several minutes. Then, as if it had taken him a while to nerve himself up to it, he reached his right arm toward Sam, rotated a little, and set the five quarters on the bar at Sam's right. "There you go, buddy," he said, and swivelled back to talk to the woman. It was a memorable incident, and sometimes Sam thought of it when he had quarters stacked on the bar and left them unattended.

Turning now with the two quarters in his right hand, he glanced again in the direction of the restaurant and caught a scowling look from Cundall. There was no waitress around this time, so Sam wondered where the look was coming from.

Back at the pool table, as he was putting the balls on the table and racking them, he motioned with his head for T.J. to come closer.

"What the hell's with that guy Cundall? He's given me a dirty look at least twice."

"Ah, don't pay any attention to him."

"I guess I shouldn't. I don't even know him. But when someone gives me a look like that, it makes me wonder."

"Ah, he's a punk."

Sam frowned. "What do you mean?"

"He's a half-assed crook, and he knows it."

"Oh?"

"Yeah, these guys all act like their ice is colder than anyone else's, but there's things to be known about 'em. This guy and Burroughs, the realtor, have done a shady deal or two, and they're being investigated for it."

"What's that have to do with me?"

"Oh, I think he's pissed at me."

"What for?"

"I think he knows I know something about what he's up to."

"Oh." Sam gave T.J. a close look. "Whose fault is that, if he did something and you know about it?"

T.J. shrugged.

"I mean, you weren't in on it, were you?"

"Nah, hell, no."

"Then what's his problem?"

"I think maybe he thinks I ratted on him."

"Why would you do that? Or, why would he think you would do that?"

T.J. gave another shrug and a little toss of the head. "I think he's pissed because I heard it from his wife."

"Oh, man. That could be kind of tight." Sam didn't want to ask if T.J. had done any informing, or why. Instead, he looked at the table of four, who were all bent over their plates. "And the other guys in their little clique, do you suppose they know?"

"About what? About the crooked deal, or about her, or what?"

"Well, any of it."

"Oh, I guess they probably all know something. And I think she might have had something to do with Arnett at some time or another, too."

Sam raised his eyebrows. "Boy, they're a fine bunch, aren't they?" He imagined what fun it would be to ride around in the Suburban with three or four of those fellows, every one of them having something on someone else.

T.J. gave what looked like a confidential smile. "Yeah. That's why I was so happy to see 'em pull in."

Sam finished racking the balls and stood by to wait for T.J.'s break shot. This was a fine kettle of fish, he thought, to be snowed in with this bunch, T.J. included.

They played through the game, with Sam scratching on the eight-ball. "I think I've had enough pool for right now," he said, sticking the cue stick back in the wall rack.

T.J. wrinkled his nose and nodded. He walked over to the juke box, which had gone silent. "What do you want to hear?"

"Hell, I don't care."

T.J. stood looking at the song titles, and after a long minute he glanced up. "Have you seen this one?" he asked, pointing at one of the jokes pinned up on the wall to the left of the juke box.

Sam shook his head and walked over. It was like hundreds of bar jokes a fellow saw plastered on the refrigerators, cigarette machines, and walls—a discolored photocopy, curling at the edges. This one read, "When I die, I want to go like my grandfather did—in his sleep. Not screaming, like the passengers in his car."

It caught Sam just right, the absurdity and the surprise. He laughed and then laughed again.

T.J. looked at him and said, "To hell with these guys. Really. Let's just have a good time."

Sam nodded and smiled. A song came out of the juke box, and by now Sam knew it well enough to sing along.

There's a salmon-colored girl
Who sets my heart a-whirl,
Who lives along the Yukon far away.

To hell with it, he thought. He didn't have anything to do with those wheeler-dealers. And they were keeping their distance.

Sam and T.J. went back to sit at the bar and kill time. Morris asked if they thought they would like to watch television, and they said no. He said the other fellows wanted to watch a football game, so he unplugged the set and carried it into the restaurant, where he set it on the counter. The four men pulled their chairs around so that they were now all out of view. Sam imagined the old couple and the two old ladies were welcome to watch football whether they wanted to or not.

At about seven o'clock, Morris said they were going to shut down the kitchen in a little while, so if the boys wanted to order something they might be thinking about it. Sam, having noticed that the pale-complexioned couple from Newcastle had ordered hot roast beef sandwiches covered with gravy, asked for that. T.J. said he would have the same. Morris went back to the kitchen and after a little while brought their order to the bar.

They drank coffee after the meal. Sam figured he had drunk at least ten beers, and he thought that might be enough. He didn't feel drunk, but he knew he had plenty of alcohol in him. Even if he didn't have to drive anywhere, he didn't want to get so bad off that he couldn't watch out for himself.

All of the people in the restaurant had come through the bar at least once in the afternoon to go to the rest rooms. Now, as the pale man from Sheridan gave a nod in passing, Sam thought it might be well to get away from the flow of traffic, so that the old ladies, who might be mortified enough at having to walk through a barroom at this time of night, would not have to walk right past the two patrons. He suggested to T.J. that they go sit in the chairs on the south wall, which they did.

At about 8:00, Morris started ushering people to their sleeping quarters. Sam and T.J. took that as their cue to go fetch their sleeping bags and overnight things from the pickup. Sam thought the two pairs of older people had been pretty good-humored about the whole situation, and their voices were cheery as they said their good-nights and went out the front door. By 8:30, Morris had the travelers settled in the trailer houses and had brought a heap of blankets to the restaurant.

Sam and T.J. sat up until all the other men had been to the rest room; then they rolled out their sleeping bags by the pool table and turned off the lights. Sam did not go to sleep right away, and it didn't sound as if T.J. did, either, but a general silence settled upon the Quadrille. Now with the lights out, the place seemed more isolated and cut off from the world than before.

It was the type of setting a person saw in a movie—the roads closed, the place sealed off with snow and cold. All they needed was for someone to cut the phone lines. That was the way it happened in the movies. Then something disastrous or terrifying took place—maybe one of the trailer houses burned down, or one of the old ladies got killed. Morris would commandeer the insurance agent's cell phone. Everyone would get rounded up in the restaurant, where they would keep an eye on one another. The stranded travelers would get a better look at one another and at the kitchen help. Sam would find out if Scott was Jackie's legitimate partner or some sinister fugitive from justice. There would be a red quarter playing in there somewhere as a clue.

Sam turned over in his sleeping bag. The floor was hard already, and it was barely 9:00 o'clock. The wind and snow had let up after sunset, but it was a cold night out there. The two antelope carcasses would be good and chilly if not frozen solid in the morning. If the storm had passed over by then, the snow plows would start out and open the roads. There was no way to hurry the process. Everyone knew that. A person just waited, and it was good to have even this much.

* * * * *

Sam awoke from a half-sleep. He had heard a voice. A little while before that—he didn't know how long—he had been aware of T.J. getting up to go the bathroom. Now he was wide awake at the sound of a voice.

He had crawled into the sleeping bag wearing his jeans and flannel shirt, so he didn't have to think about whether to get dressed. He sat up and eased out of the bag, then turned and pulled on his hunting boots. Without lacing them he walked toward the rest room, trying not to make any sound.

He heard a voice again, not T.J.'s, when he was a couple of steps away from the door. Then he heard nothing. He paused for a couple of seconds, wondering if he should wait to go in, and then he decided he did not want to overhear anything or give anyone a chance to do anything that could have been avoided. He took two more steps and pushed open the rest room door.

The bright light made him squint, but he saw what he had expected. Cundall had followed T.J. to the can. They stood about eight feet apart—T.J. with his back to the urinal and facing the door, Cundall with his back to the door but now half-turned to see who had barged in.

It was a long moment there in the harsh light. T.J.'s dark wavy hair and dark eyes matched the unflinching look on his face. If someone had come to push him around, it hadn't gone very far. Cundall, who was taller than average, struck an overbearing pose as he stood with his right hand in the pocket of his camouflage hunting parka. He had trim brown hair and went clean-shaven, but he had a dark beard that was well past the five-o'clock shadow. It emphasized the heavy, sullen look he had put on, but his expression did not have as much force as his earlier scowls did. He was standing in the bright light of a men's room, where he had stalked one man and had been caught at it by another.

Sam felt it in the air. The guy had lost some of his swagger. When the intimidation wasn't private, he couldn't work it as well. Sam waited, and it didn't take much longer for things to change.

Cundall took his hand out of his coat pocket and let it hang by his side. Then, after one last glowering look at T.J., he turned and walked past Sam without looking at him, pulled the door open, and left.

Sam let out a long breath. "What the hell was that all about?"

T.J. tipped a glance at the door. "I don't know. I just came in here to take a leak."

"He must have been waiting for you to get up."

"I imagine."

"It sure seemed to me like he had a pistol in his pocket."

"I wouldn't be surprised. But I think he would have had a hell of a time using it."

Sam wagged his eyebrows. "You don't know how a guy like that thinks."

"No, but whatever he might have thought he could do, that's gone. He got caught with his dick hangin' out."

"Yeah, I suppose so." Sam looked in the direction of the door, then back at T.J. He shook his head and walked out.

Back in his sleeping bag, Sam did not relax until T.J. returned. Then, even when it sounded as if everyone else had settled down, Sam did not go to sleep right away. It had been quite an encounter in the men's room. Cundall would have to remember it as a moment when two guys he looked down on had his number. And T.J. would have to remember it as a moment in which things might not have worked out so well for him. For all of his carefree attitude of hoisting a cool one and singing "Squaws Along the Yukon," he would have to think about the danger of a fellow like Cundall every once in a while.

Sam turned over in his bed. The cement floor had no give to it. He thought about how things would be at breakfast—ten people drinking coffee and clattering forks and knives, and at least three of them knowing about a long moment of tension in the glare of the rest room. Breakfast would go on, and all the other travelers would be cheerful about having gotten through the night. At some point the snow plows would come, and the ten people would get into their various vehicles and drive away.

Sam thought about the scenarios he had imagined earlier—a trailer burning down, one of the old people getting killed, a gathering of the suspects. Funny stuff. But the moment with Cundall was real. Sam was glad the man didn't get a chance to make things worse.

He thought about Morris, the genial owner. Morris would be a good character to confiscate the cell phone or pounce on the red quarter as a clue, and he might even be amused if Sam told him of the role he had cast for him. Sam knew he wouldn't tell him, but he was sure that if Morris knew of either the imagined scenarios or the real one, he would be very happy that nothing unsavory had taken place on that one cold night at the Quadrille.

On the Outskirts

On the first morning after he got home from jail, Tom saddled his horse and took a ride down the back side of the ridge, across country, to see if he could catch a glimpse of Loretta. It was shorter to cut across on horseback than it was to drive around in the pickup. It was less noticeable, too.

When he got to the line of elms, there was a big gap in the picture. The trailer house was plumb gone. Tom rode up to take a closer look.

There was a large bare spot sixteen feet wide and sixty feet long where the trailer had been yanked out—skirting, blocks, anchors, and all. The water supply line and an electrical cable poked up out of the ground near where the back door had been. A dirty scrap of carpet was draped over the sewer hook-up. The front steps still stood in place, anchored in cement and leading up to nothing but mid-air. Except for a few splinters of wood, a plastic broom, and one dark blue sock, the spot was clean. A fringe of last year's grass grew around the edge of the cleared area. Other than that, it was just bare ground and a set of steps leading to nowhere.

He rode the horse across the empty spot. Only a week earlier, there had been a large solid object right here, and now there was nothing. Just pulled up and gone. He stopped the horse short of the steps, at about the spot where the couch used to be. The horse dropped some road apples, and Tom dismounted to take a leak.

He imagined Loretta sitting on the couch, smoking a cigarette, watching television or working a crossword puzzle, and maybe doing her nails—three feet in the air, all hooked up somewhere else. Gordon must feel pretty damn smug about this one. Tom swung into the saddle, reined around, and rode back across the bedroom.

* * * * *

From the window he could look down the slope and see the bare upper branches of the fruit trees, and beyond them, the lower half of the horse pasture, close-cropped and drab in winter, ending at the fence on the south where the weeds grew tall beyond the horse's reach. On cold mornings the coyotes came hunting, sometimes five in a pack, entering the pasture from the east and crossing below the fruit trees, finding nothing as they headed for the gully and deep grass to the west. Good luck to them. Tom's gaze returned to the line of trees halfway down the slope, girdling the hillside like a belt. With a wild plum thicket on the left end, six apple trees evenly spaced, then a plum tree and the clump of chokecherries, it was a narrow fertile island. Fenced in from the grassland, the line of trees followed the route of an old irrigation ditch that ran water no more, not since the previous owner had sold the water rights. With shovel and hoe, Tom had widened the strip into a terrace, fifteen feet across, then with his back to the native plums had planted the trees. For the first few years he had caught overflow from the diversion gate, but then the ditch rider noticed it, and that was the end of the reason Tom planted the trees there to begin with. Now any water they got came from his efforts alone.

He could recall the countless times he had stood in the wide space between two apple trees and had thought of how he would pitch the tent when Loretta came. But Loretta never came, not long enough for that, and it turned out, like so many other things, to be something they just talked about. Now he was not talking to Loretta at all but had begun to talk to another woman, Isabel, who lived farther north than Loretta did in the south, and he wondered how close he would ever get to her. From the bedroom where he stood, he could barely see the tops of the smallest trees. Between any two of the dwarf apples there was still room for a tent. And there was no danger of getting wet.

* * * * *

On the Fourth of July, Tom was obliged to clean up some cat feces under his work bench in the garage. It looked as if the black-and-white cat had crossed the line.

For the past month, Tom had smelled cat urine in and around the garage and had seen where a cat had pissed on the door and on the foundation of the garage. From time to time in the morning as he looked out the kitchen window, he had seen a black cat with a white chest, and on a couple of occasions in the evening he had heard a ruckus in the garage. Each time when he went out, the yellow cat was crouched near the feed dish, and a black cat was slipping away through the pet door.

Tom hadn't killed a cat for about three years, since he had had to deal with a white-and-tan one that was terrorizing the cat food and making phantasmal appearances in the night. It had been a messy business, and he decided that having to rub out stray cats was a way of accepting someone else's problems. Now, though, he was beginning to think that he might have to take measures against the black-and-white cat.

Later the same day, on the Fourth, as he was drinking a glass of water at the kitchen sink, he saw the cat strolling through the cedar trees. Tom went for the rifle, but when he came back, he couldn't find the animal. He set the rifle in the laundry room and went about sharpening a kitchen knife. After about five minutes, as he looked out the window, he saw the cat strolling down the driveway toward the power pole.

Taking quiet steps to the laundry room, Tom fetched the .22; he went to the front room, opened the storm door, and got a good aim. The cat paused to look around and then turned to walk forward. Tom zeroed in on the side of its head and took a shot. The cat went right down, flopped around, and settled.

Tom walked out into the sunlight, and as he approached the cat he observed the neat hole he had made by the left ear. With the rifle barrel he lifted up the cat's hind leg, and there, sure enough, was a round pair of balls encased in a layer of solid black fur.

It reminded Tom of a moment many years earlier, when his father had killed a cat. He said he didn't like doing things like that, but sometimes it was necessary. Then he tipped back the leg and explained the source of trouble. He told Tom what balls were, what purpose they served, and why people removed them from cats and horses.

That was the trouble with the black cat, all right. If Tom had a son, he could tell him about it.

* * * * *

Tom got a good rest on the fencepost and put the crosshairs on the front quarter. The deer stood out as a dark spot against the mottled pale-and-green alfalfa. In the fading light, the antlers were just visible as the buck made slight movements in its grazing.

Tom took a slow breath to calm himself as he calculated his chances. He was shooting across the fence onto a neighboring field, the day after the season ended, but he had a steady aim. He was sure the deer didn't know the difference of time or place either one, and the people who did were mostly inside with their windows closed. One shot at dusk was not likely to attract much notice.

The deer stepped forward, turned to the right, then straightened out again and gave a good profile. With the crosshairs settled again, Tom squeezed the trigger.

The rifle shot crashed in the cold air, louder to him as he knew where he stood. Then the sound was gone, and the deer was down. Tom walked back up the draw to his house, wending his way through sagebrush, careful not to make any quick motions to draw attention.

After putting his rifle away, he went down the slope again with his tow-rope. He could see a fringe of snow along the line of weeds at the fence line, but the hayfield itself wouldn't show sprinkles of blood or tracks from the dragging.

When he had the deer back under his own fence and onto his pasture, he went for the wheelbarrow. Dusk had closed in, and his movements would be hard to pick out at any distance. Tipping the wheelbarrow on its side and reaching over to grab the deer by a front and back leg, he flopped the animal and settled the cart upright. Then he lifted the head where it hung over the front and touched the tire. He tucked the antlers under the right shoulder, which lay upside, and had the dead weight centered.

It was going to be a long push, and he had had a good burst of exertion already from dragging the animal, but he was not tired as he took the handles. He had done what he set out to do. As for going uphill, alone in the falling dark, he was used to it.

* * * * *

When Tom went out to check on his horse on Saturday morning, the animal was stiff and cold. The night before, he had to coax the horse onto its feet, and now it was never going to rise again. Snowflakes and clots of sleet were falling on the sorrel coat and not melting. With the ground frozen as it was, Tom knew he couldn't bury the horse if he wanted.

He walked up the hill and made a few phone calls. First he located a pet products company and arranged to have a truck come and pick up the carcass. After that, he talked with a couple of veterinarians he knew well enough to call. They both told him, based on what he said, that the horse had probably twisted an intestine while rolling in the dirt and then necrosis had set in. Necrosis, necrotic—words to describe something that went on inside before Tom could have known to do anything. Words to make sense of things gone wrong.

The truck showed up in the latter part of the morning. Tom heard it first and then saw it, white and clean, not brown or rust-colored like the old tallow trucks. Pet products—the woman on the phone had told him to have fifty dollars ready.

The driver, a dark man with a light-featured woman to keep him company, drove down into the pasture and backed up to the horse. He raised the tilt bed, lowered the end gate, reached in and pulled out a shiny chain, and wrapped it around the horse's front leg. A motor started turning; the chain tightened and then clunked as it slipped into place on the winch. The stiff horse moved up onto the tailgate ramp, made a cold thump as it rolled over in the steel box, and settled into place with three bloated calves, all black.

As Tom handed him the fifty-dollar bill, the driver said, "I'm sorry for your loss." He let down the bed, closed the end gate, got into the cab where the woman was waiting, and made out a receipt. After giving the slip to Tom, he climbed into the cab again and drove away. On the receipt he had written, "Red horse."

Tom walked up the hill, and as he closed the pasture gate he could see the clean white truck pulling out onto the highway.

A phrase played through his mind, something his father used to say. "Saddle your own horses." Even when the horse was stone dead and a guy with a winch and a chain hauled him away, things couldn't be much clearer than that.

Campers

As I pulled around the last bend in the road before getting to camp, my headlights swept across a silver-grey pickup with a pop-up camper. It looked like Overby's. A hundred yards further I turned off the main road into the camping spot, which isn't a developed campground but just a level area big enough for half a dozen outfits. A second look at the camper and pickup left no doubt as to whose it was. Sometimes I would go weeks or even months without talking to Hollis and Overby, and then we would run into each other at elk camp, just as normal as if we were neighbors in town.

Overby's pickup sat in the spot that would be my first choice if I could have it, so I pulled in across from him, with the tail end of my camper facing the tail end of his. As I got out of the cab, the door to his camper opened, spilling light into the darkness.

"Is that you, Ray?"

"It sure is. Are you by yourself, Russ?"

"Just me and a couple of sixteen-year-old runaway girls."

"That's good," I said. "Let me get my things straightened out, and I'll come over."

"I'll be here," he said, and closed the door.

I let down the tailgate and crawled into my camper. The air was cold, especially after I'd been sitting in the warm cab for the last three hours. I dug out my propane lantern and lit it, then laid out my kitchen box, duffel bag, and bedroll the way I like them. Between the little bit of heat that the lantern put out and the heat I worked up by moving around, my camper felt less like an icebox. I had picked up a hamburger and fries in Laramie and had eaten on the road, but I was hungry again, so I ate a granola bar and drank a cup of water. It wasn't even nine o'clock yet. I was in no hurry to go inhale Overby's cigarette smoke, but there were a couple of things I wanted to sound him out about.

The pickup tailgate was cold to the touch as I let myself onto the ground, so I put on my gloves as I walked across the ruts that ran through the campground. I knew it would be warm inside Overby's camper, and I supposed he would have a bottle of Windsor Canadian set out for company. As for the two runaway girls, I imagined they were figments of his humor, which ranged from irreverent to heartless.

His voice sounded before I was close enough to knock. "Come on in."

I stepped onto the wooden box and up to the tailgate, then opened the door. A rush of light and warmth and cigarette odor met me. Overby sat at the table, his full head of hair and neatly trimmed beard showing the first signs of silver in the lamp light.

"Mr. Decker," he said, nodding.

"Mr. Overby." I nodded back. "Shall I sit down?"

"Please do." He set a plastic glass in front of me, then slid the bottle next to it. "Go ahead. I just poured myself one."

I looked at the empty glass. "Ice?"

He motioned his thumb toward the icebox, which was built into the cabinets of his camper.

I got some ice into the cup and poured in some whisky, then went to the tap for water. The pump motor hummed beneath the sinkboard as I mixed my drink.

"What time did you get in?" I sat down across from him at the little table.

"Just at dark."

"Where are the girls?"

His blue eyes sparkled. "They're in the bedroom, freshening up."

I glanced up at his bunk, which had a sleeping bag rolled out with a winter coat on top of it. I looked back at him and said, "How do they do that?"

Overby gave a tight smile. "I don't always know. I remember one time a whore in Nevada said she had to freshen up, and when I walked into the room, I could tell she'd smoked a joint."

"No tellin' what those girls are up to, then."

Overby shook out a cigarette. "They know I'll spank 'em if they do anything bad."

Thinking we'd ridden that joke long enough, I didn't say anything for a moment as I poked at the ice in my drink. Then I said, "Any idea of whether the elk are in here?"

"Not really. Not yet." Overby lit the cigarette. "What kind of a permit do you have?"

"Cow." I sipped my drink. It tasted sweet and cold and strong.

"Mine's general."

"So you've got to shoot something with horns, and I've got to shoot something without."

"Uh-huh. Of course, if you see a bull, don't be shy. I'll put my tag on him."

I nodded. Overby liked to party-hunt, so that either guy could cover what the other one would shoot. I hadn't ever gotten anything with him that way, so it was mainly just talk. It was hard to say I didn't want to hunt on the buddy system, so I just said, "Sounds O.K. to me."

We sat for a moment without talking until he asked how I did with deer and antelope.

"I got an antelope but I haven't gotten a deer yet. How about you?"

"I got both."

"Uh-huh. I thought that was what Hollis said."

His eyes flickered. "Oh. Yeah."

I pictured Hollis as I had seen him last, in the dim light of the Pastime Club, his balding head and lean, shaved face in half-shadows. "Yeah. He said he didn't know if he would make it but I might see you up here."

"Well, he was right again, wasn't he?" Overby smiled as he took a drag on his cigarette.

"He sure was." I thought for a second about one of the things I had in mind. "I had a funny little run-in at the Wetmore Ranch, and I asked him about it."

"Oh, yeah?" Overby ashed his cigarette.

"Uh-huh. I stopped there and asked for permission to hunt antelope, and Wetmore wouldn't let me. He seemed pretty pissed. He said he'd had too much trouble with hunters already, and he wasn't letting anyone else hunt this year."

Overby raised his eyebrows but didn't say anything.

"I know you guys hunt out there, and I got permission a couple of years ago, so I thought I'd give it a try."

"But he just turned you away, huh?"

"Uh-huh. I told him all I was looking for was an antelope, but he didn't want to talk about it. I wondered what his problem was, with a measly antelope tag. Everyone I know would just as soon thin 'em out, and as far as that's concerned, I went on to Shoemaker's and got my antelope without any problem anyway."

"Well, I think he did have some trouble."

"That's what Hollis told me. He said Wetmore was mad because someone shot one of his cows."

"That's what Steve told you?"

"Yeah."

"Well, I think it was Steve that did it, and it was a bull. A Black Angus bull."

I let out a breath and looked at my drink. I wondered if Hollis had really done something like that. If he had, he must have been too embarrassed to say it. "Well," I said, "I guess Wetmore had a right to get good and mad."

"Oh, no doubt." Overby took another pull on his cigarette.

I looked up at him. "What kind of a dumb-ass move was it to shoot someone's cow? or bull?"

Overby's eyebrows went up again. "Steve just hasn't had his head on straight since his wife left him."

That stopped me for a second. It was the other thing I wanted to find out about, and I couldn't just come out and ask. So I said, "He did seem to be a little down about it."

Overby shrugged. "Anyone would be."

I decided to go a little further. "I guess so. Kim's a pretty nice woman."

He sniffed. "Even if she was an ugly bitch, it would go rough on a guy."

"Uh-huh." I looked at Overby, who was looking at his cigarette as he set it in the ashtray. I couldn't tell a thing by the way he was acting. But I believed what my ex-wife had told me. She said Overby had seen her in the Blue Light Lounge and had hinted at her enough that she felt he was hitting on her. On top of that, she said, Overby had been sneaking around with Kim Hollis.

"Seems to me like he wants to get next to all of his friends' ex-wives," she said.

Looking at him, I believed what Barb had told me. Overby was an opportunist, the kind of guy that liked to find his way into places where he thought the voltage was a little higher. In that moment I despised him, but I couldn't see a way to open the subject any more. "Too bad," I said. "I went through it, and I didn't think it would happen to me. But it did."

Overby picked up his drink for the first time since I had come in. "It could happen to anyone."

I doubted that he meant it all the way. I had heard how his own wife had tried to leave and he had bullied her out of it. But I hadn't heard it from him, so I didn't say anything.

He set his drink down. "Did he tell you how we almost froze to death up here?"

"No. When was that?"

"Just last weekend."

"Really?"

"Yeah. It got colder than hell. It was nice and warm in here, but when we went out in the morning, it was so cold that your fingers ached, even with your gloves on."

"He didn't tell me about that."

"Not much to it, really, except that he got goofy on me."

"How was that?"

"Well, we walked up on that first ridge, which is a pretty steep climb, and he sort of ran out of gas. So rather than split up, I had him stay with me. He got kind of bleary-eyed, and he stumbled along. When things warmed up he took his gloves off and lost one of 'em, and poked the barrel of his gun in the snow, and slipped on the trail a couple of times. When we got down to the bottom, he was so woozy he couldn't walk back out. I had to come back by myself, take down my camper, and put everything away so I could drive down and get him."

I shook my head. "He didn't mention it. He just said he didn't care if he went out again this year." I looked at Overby. "Do you think he's all right?"

"Oh, yeah. He just weakened, that's all. He let all the shit get to him, and it knocked his chemistry out of whack."

We drifted into another subject and chatted on for a little while. I finished my drink and thanked him for it, then stepped out into the cold night.

Back in my camper, I got my lantern going again. I could see my own breath, and I sat with my hat, coat, and gloves on as I thought about what I would need in the morning. I took my vest out of the duffel bag and made sure it had the padded pouch of rifle shells. I checked for the survival items, also—matches, flashlight, granola bars, extra gloves. I looked at the clock. It was twenty to ten, time for bed. I decided to go out for a leak, then come back in and go to bed.

Overby's camper still had light shining in it. It was like a fortress, I thought. Overby the invincible. His comment about Hollis reminded me of a line he liked to use in the bar, when everyone had had a few. "It's a good life," he would say, "if you don't weaken."

I went back into my camper and made short work of getting into my sleeping bag. As I lay in the dark I could hear the clock ticking and the lantern cooling off. I wondered how cold it would be in the morning.

I heard the noise of Overby's camper door, once as he went out and once as he went back in. I remembered a story we had all laughed about. There were two schoolteachers, up in Gillette, who worked together and were friends. They made the statewide news when one of them found his wife in the other man's camper, out at some roadside rest. The husband aimed his pistol at the guy's genitals, but he botched it and shot him in the leg. Of course the guy in the camper said he was just talking to the woman, with his pants off. That incident happened well before Hollis or I had our marital problems and a while after Overby squelched his, so it was good for a few laughs.

After that there was another story come down from Gillette. This time it was two fellows who worked at a big coal mine. One of them found out the other was having an affair with his wife, who worked in the offices at the mine. So the jealous husband hid in the other man's car, with a hunting rifle, and killed him on the way home from work. Then he drove the vehicle and dead man back to the mine, where he used some of the big equipment to crush and bury the outfit.

That got some laughs, too, about how all those people in Gillette carried on. Overby said the guy at the mine went about it better than the schoolteacher did. At least he had the right equipment.

As I lay there after hearing Overby go out and then back in, I wondered how many women, if any, he had had in his camper. He had so little regard for other people's problems and so much confidence in himself that he wouldn't worry about someone with a pistol knocking on the door. I knew there were people like him, brazen, who always seemed to be at the top of their game and didn't meet with any consequences. At least on the surface, they seemed to have everything they needed, and they didn't seem to have disruptions.

Then I remembered another story, maybe ten years before the schoolteacher story, when a hunter up in the Big Horns killed three other elk hunters. According to the guy's story, the three men—two brothers from Greybull and their friend from North Dakota—jumped him when he went to their camp to take back something they had stolen from him. I imagined a shoot-out in an elk camp, three against one, and I supposed it would take some nerve to be able to kill three men like that. The guy went to trial twice and then went free. The kicker to the story was that a couple of years later, he drowned in a reservoir down in Sweetwater County, when he was out on the water with his wife and kids. The newspaper article was interesting to read. It just told about his drowning and about his killing the other three men, and it left it up to the reader to decide whether there was some moral of higher justice. That was the way I took it, that he got his after all.

I thought about Hollis and whether he had the desire to punish Overby, and if so, whether he had the right equipment. I sort of doubted it, he seemed so ineffective, but I knew a person couldn't always tell.

Then I wondered if Overby would ever get his come-uppance in some other way. I thought it unlikely that I would read about him drowning, or freezing to death, but then again, the guy who drowned probably surprised the people who knew him. I would imagine he seemed like one of those sons of bitches that always got away with their maneuvers.

Overby in his snug camper. I wondered if he had a vulnerable spot, if anything would ever bring him down, by accident or by the right equipment. I figured it was more than a person could hope for, and only time would tell.

In the middle of the night I heard a vehicle pull in and park by Overby's camper. I heard voices, and one of them sounded like Hollis. I was warm in my sleeping bag and didn't want to disturb my nest by sitting up, so I just turned over and stayed put. Why Hollis would come up in the middle of the night rather than ride with Overby to begin with was a bit of an odd question, but it didn't keep me awake for long.

My alarm clock started clanging at five-thirty. It was cold and dark inside my camper until I fired up my lantern. Once as I was fixing coffee I looked over and saw a light in

Overby's camper. Well enough, I thought. After that I heard someone open the camper door and close it, open a pickup door and close it, and then go back into the camper. A couple of minutes later I heard a shot.

I looked at the burner beneath the coffee pot. It always took a long time to get coffee going on cold mornings, so I decided to leave the stove and lantern burning while I climbed out to see what was going on.

As I walked across the way, I could see Hollis's pickup, the blue Ford. I took soft steps until I was within a couple of yards of Overby's camper. I thought of hollering out a blunt question of whether everyone was alive, but I thought better of it and just asked if everything was all right.

Overby's voice came back. "Yeah. Come on in."

I stepped up onto the tail gate and opened the door to the camper. Overby sat at the right side of the table, and Hollis sat across from him. Smoke curled up from two cigarettes in the ashtray.

"Who touched off the cannon?" I asked.

Hollis, with his balding head lowered, looked up at me. "I did. I brought it in here where it was warm, to load it, and I had one in the chamber that I didn't know was there."

I looked from him to Overby, who had the sort of calm, superior look a person was entitled to have when someone else was the idiot.

"Any damage?" I asked.

Overby made a backward motion with his head. "Put a little hole in the wall next to the closet, was all."

I looked at Hollis. "Are you all right, Steve?"

He nodded. "Oh, yeah. Just scared the hell out of me."

I turned toward Overby, who seemed to be enjoying the moment. "Well," I said, "I left my stove on. I just came over to see if anybody got hurt."

Overby lifted his cigarette to his lips and shook his head.

I paused for a second. "Are you guys goin' to hunt over west from here?"

Overby exhaled his smoke. "I think so."

"Well, good luck, then. I hope you get an elk."

Hollis looked up. "Thanks. Same to you, Ray."

I went back to my camper, had my cereal and then coffee, and started out on my hunt without stopping by to check with the other two. I had decided to hunt the big ridge in back of camp on the northeast. It was always a long, solitary hunt, the kind I liked. The first grey was starting to show in the sky, but I knew I had time to get to the top to watch the sun rise.

As I found the trail and hiked off through the trees, I heard the door to Overby's camper open and close. Maybe it was like a ship, with Overby the captain and Hollis the cabin boy. I wondered again if anyone would ever find Overby's weak spot, and I was pretty sure that if anyone did, it wouldn't be Hollis. They made a better pair than I might have imagined. I put my thumb under the sling strap of my rifle, and as I started my uphill climb, I thought of what a nice view I would get from the top of the ridge.

Dead Man's Gun

Rory was heading west into the late afternoon sun, following a dump truck that had a heap of rubble showing above the tailgate. As he edged over to see if he could pass, he saw a white car about half a mile away and coming in his direction. He sagged back and let the dump truck pull ahead. Rory settled into watching the tail end of the vehicle, until he saw movement on the right. A brown-speckled steer came up out of the ditch on the north side of the road and stepped onto the pavement to cross behind the truck. Rory hit the brakes. He was sure the steer was going to walk into the other lane in front of the white car, and he braced himself for what might happen.

As the truck cleared away and the white car came into view, the animal stepped into the car's lane. The driver swerved, hitting the steer in the hind quarter and knocking it aside; then, with his eyes widened, he cut to his left across the highway in front of Rory and came to a stop nose-down in the ditch. Though it all happened in a flash, Rory noticed that the car was an older-model Ford and that the driver, a man with long hair and a mustache, was alone.

With the steer going one way and the car another, Rory's pickup was unscathed. He had hit the brakes twice to keep from going into a skid, and now as he brought it to a complete stop, he was even with the steer, which was slumped downhill on the roadside to his left. The car sat a little ways back on his right. Rory put the pickup into motion again, moved it to the edge of the road, and set the flasher. Then he got out to see how the driver of the car was doing.

The man was on his feet, looking across the top of the car in Rory's direction.

"Son of a bitch came out of nowhere."

"Yeah, it all happened just like that. He came up out of the ditch. Are you all right?"

The man nodded. "I'm all right. How about the cow?"

"It looks deader'n a mackerel."

The man came up onto the shoulder. "What the hell was it doin' on the road?"

"I'd guess it was going back to the feedlot."

The man looked at his car. "Well, I guess I'm stuck here."

"Do you want me to try to pull you out?"

"I don't know." He looked across the highway where the dead steer lay. "I sure can't go anywhere till we get this thing reported, and if I move anything, it'll just give someone something to complain about."

Rory had a good look at the man by now. He was a little above average height, with long brown hair parted in the middle, a mustache that grew past the corners of his mouth, and brown eyes that moved but did not shift. He had broad shoulders and a deep chest, but he was not bulky. Rather, he was lean and trim in a white t-shirt and a pair of faded jeans. He had a hard look to him; he seemed like the type of fellow that troublesome things happened to, and when they did, he took his knocks.

The man drew a pack of Winstons and an orange-colored lighter from his shirt pocket. His arm showed muscle as he rapped a cigarette against the lighter, then put it in his mouth and lit it. "Have you got a cell phone?"

"No, I don't." Rory looked at the dump truck, almost a mile away by now. "Just about everyone else does, though. I imagine there'll be someone come along in a few minutes."

The man blew away a stream of smoke. "You live around here?"

"A couple of miles out."

A nod, a glance at Rory's pickup, as if to gauge how far apart the two of them were.

"Yourself?"

"I live in town." He looked at his car. "I don't need this kind of shit. No one does."

Rory shrugged. He figured the guy meant the cops. "Well, I'm sorry it happened. If it'll do any good, I'll be glad to be a witness. I mean, you couldn't have done anything else. I could say that much."

The man moved his head up and down a couple of times, then looked at Rory and said, "Could you do me a favor?"

"I guess it depends on what it is."

Silence hung for a few seconds. "I've got a gun, that if they find it on me, they'll take it. What if we just put it in your gun rack?"

"A rifle?"

"Yeah."

"It's not stolen, is it?"

"No, not really. I got it in a deal. It's just that I'm on probation, and the first thing they'll do is look through my car. Then it's my ass in the sling."

Rory looked up and down the highway. "What kind of gun is it?"

"Nothin' fancy." The man walked downhill through the weeds, opened the rear door on the passenger's side, and motioned with his head.

Rory sidestepped down the slope and looked into the back of the car. Lying on a jumble of clothing, where it had apparently slid off the seat and onto the transmission hump, was a lever-action carbine with no sling or scope. He nodded.

The long-haired man reached in and drew out the rifle.

"Looks like a .30-30," Rory said.

"It is."

The rifle looked clean and simple as the sunlight cast a dull shine on it. "Do you want me to keep it for you, then, or do you want to try to get something for it? I mean, I'm not really in the market for another gun."

"Just take it for right now, and we'll talk about it later." The man straightened up, shifted the rifle to his left hand, and held out his right. "I'm Danny Lejeune."

"I'm Rory Anderson." He took the rifle and climbed to the passenger's side of his pickup, where he scanned up and down the highway. He opened the door and poked the .30-30 into the gun rack.

Danny Lejeune stood beside him. "As soon as someone shows up with a cell phone, you can take off if you want."

"You don't need me to be a witness?" Rory looked across the road at the dead steer.

"I'm not too worried about that part. If you want to stay around long enough to talk to the cop, I guess that's all right, too. It's your call."

"I'll do it that way, then."

Rory didn't see Danny Lejeune for a while. From time to time he saw the .30-30 in his gun closet and wondered what sort of use the guy had for that type of firearm. It was a hunting rifle, the kind that some people called a brush gun, fine for close range but not much good for deer and antelope in this country. It made a handy saddle gun or a general knock-around rifle, something to keep in the gun rack if a fellow was out on thc rangeland and needed to take a crack at something. Danny Lejeune sure didn't look like a cowboy or a ranch hand, and he didn't seem to have the reluctance that a hunter would have if he had to give up a rifle. He said he had gotten it in a deal. Rory figured it was just a piece of property to him, something small and portable that kept its value. If it had been his for very long, and if he had a use for it, he would do something to get it back. It wouldn't be hard. He had Rory's name and could find him in the phone book, and he knew his pickup as well.

Meanwhile, Rory kept a lookout for the white Ford with the crumpled front right fender, but he did not see it. One morning when he was on his way to work, he saw Danny Lejeune riding a bicycle and carrying a lunch box. It looked as if he was on his way to work at one of the shops in the industrial park south of town. A couple of weeks later, on a

Sunday afternoon, he saw Danny riding on the passenger side of a light blue Ford pickup, an older model driven by an Indian-looking fellow with glasses and long, tied-back hair. The Ford was pulling up to the package window at the liquor store. On both occasions, there was no convenient way to stop and talk. Rory told himself that one of the next times he saw Danny, he was going to take the trouble to start a conversation with him.

The opportunity did not come up. The next time Rory knew anything of Danny Lejeune, he was reading it on the front page of the newspaper. Danny had died in a motorcycle accident when he was on a Sunday morning ride with some of his friends. According to the article, the motorcycle belonged to a person named Byron Sweetgrass, and Danny's driver's license was suspended. He was thirty-five.

On an inside page of the same newspaper, Rory found the obituary. It said Danny had two sisters, one who lived in town and one who lived in Kansas, plus a mother in Glendive, Montana. He was preceded in death by his father and one brother.

After reading the article and the obituary, Rory was left to wonder why Danny was on probation and why his license was suspended. Things like that were never mentioned in obituaries in the town paper. Even a man who died in a gunfight with the police was represented as having "died in his home." As for the article, Rory assumed that the reporter gave whatever information was pertinent to the accident, and since no one else had been hurt and no other laws had been broken, the reporter saw fit to mention the suspended license and leave it at that. The light touch. Let the public remember what it might and draw its own conclusions.

For the next several days, Rory found himself thinking about Danny Lejeune, this man he had barely met. That he had had so little in his obituary struck Rory as being tight, though he couldn't say on whose part. Even confirmed drunks he had known, who died in their fifties or early sixties, got a comment about how they liked to hunt and fish and enjoyed spending time with their grandchildren. But Danny went out of this life traveling about as light as anybody Rory had known. Or at least he seemed that way. Rory imagined him in a t-shirt and jeans, on a borrowed motorcycle, with not so much as a driver's license in his wallet, and next to nothing for anyone to say about him.

Of course there was more to it than that. There would be in anyone's case, even the humpback who worked at the wrecking yard. Danny had a couple of sisters and at least one friend. And he must have had some personal effects in addition to the rifle he never got around to reclaiming.

A little over a week after he read about Danny in the newspaper, Rory sorted out some gear to go camping for a weekend. As he did, he saw the .30-30 in the closet and wondered again if Danny ever had any use for it or if he even enjoyed the outdoors. Maybe once in a blue moon he went on a motorcycle run with some pals, but he didn't seem like the type to go to the mountains for a few days or to set aside a weekend in October to hunt deer and antelope. To the contrary, he seemed like a hard man with a tough way of life, and if he had ever had call for a gun, it would be the type he could slip under the seat.

* * * * *

After a late hailstorm and an early frost, the fall weather began to set in with a slow, cold rain. The man who sold hunting licenses in his gun shop said it was going to be an early winter. Then he told the same story he had told the year before, how he had shot a small buck antelope at six hundred yards on the last afternoon of the season, then had given the meat to a poor family he knew. Yeah, it was going to be an early winter, he said again. You could tell by the fur on the caterpillars. Hell, you could just feel it.

That night, Rory put on a felt hat and a warm canvas coat and went downtown. In recent years he didn't go to the bar during hunting season because he didn't like to be bleary-eyed and fuzzy-headed in the morning, and he could sit in a lonely camp way off in the mountains and think of the honky-tonks without feeling he was missing anything. But on the last weekend before the season opened, he could indulge himself.

A crowd had begun to gather in the Longhorn. He found a lone stool on the corner of the bar and settled in. Two women sat to his right, talking to one another. When the nearest one, a heavy-set blonde, got up to dance and stayed out on the floor, the other one fell into small talk with Rory.

She was an average-looking woman, probably in her early thirties, with straight, light brown hair and an uneven complexion. She was wearing a purple sweat shirt and faded blue jeans, and she looked a little overweight. She had a friendly smile and quick eyes, and after some preliminary conversation she moved over to her friend's stool. She scooted her cigarettes and bottle of beer with her.

Her name was Shawna and she had two kids, who were spending the weekend with their dad. She had worked at the mini-mart until it closed down, and she was between jobs right now.

Rory told her about his own job, weighing trucks and running a forklift. "But it's work. And it's not bad. You take what comes along, you know."

"I guess."

"Of course, I know I've got it easy, compared to some. For one thing, I've got a job."

"That's something. Married?"

He shook his head.

"Kids?"

"No. I've missed out on that, so far. But at least I don't have court orders and child support."

"Not that that always gets everyone to pay."

"Oh, uh-huh. I guess that makes things rough, too."

"He's an asshole, all right. He can take them out for pizza and act like the hero, and leave me strung out for the rest of it."

"That's too bad."

"It's just something else to deal with." She lit a cigarette.

"Yeah, take it in stride. Like a fella told me once, enjoy the interval. Life's too short."

"That's for damn sure. And most of the time, it sucks."

The downer attitude seemed to be at odds with the smile that came and went. After a few more minutes of conversation, she said she had been in a piss-poor mood for the last couple of months, what with the usual crap from her ex, and the mini-mart closing down, and then on top of that, she had a brother die.

"Oh, really? Who was that?"

"His name was Danny Lejeune."

"Jeez. I knew him. Not very well, but I did meet him. Just a couple of months before he . . . had his accident."

"He was a hell of a good guy." Shawna's eyes moistened, and she turned toward the beer in front of her.

"I met him the day he hit the steer on the highway. I was sorry to read about him later, in the paper."

"He died doing what he loved to do," she said, in a tone that sounded as if she had taught herself to say it.

"Well, I was sure sorry. I thought I'd get a chance to talk to him again sometime."

"You met him when he hit the cow?"

"Yeah. It happened right in front of me. I stopped, and I stayed there till the cops came."

Shawna turned and looked full at Rory. "He told me about you. He said there was a real decent guy that stopped and helped."

"I didn't really do much."

"He didn't say what you did. He just said you helped him."

"Mainly, I stuck around to tell the cops what I saw, that it wasn't his fault at all."

"Well, he appreciated it. He said you were a real decent guy. I remember those were his words."

"He seemed like a good guy to me, too."

"He was the best. Of course, he was my brother, so I'm bound to say that."

"Uh-huh. And I was sorry to read about him later."

"He died doing what he loved to do." She turned to her beer again.

As the night wore on, Shawna's girlfriend fell into closer company with the man she was dancing with, and Shawna's gloom seemed to lift. She drank her beer and a couple more, smiled, and put her hand on Rory's arm as she talked. A couple of times when the conversation came around to Danny, she drew her eyebrows together and nodded, saying, "You were his friend."

When the bar closed, Rory bought a six-pack to go and drove Shawna to her place. She lived in a mobile home in a small court on the west side of town. He parked his pickup by the front steps, then waited next to her in the cold, damp air as she fumbled for her keys.

Once inside, they drank about half a beer each in the living room and then went to the bedroom, where in the glow of a night light he saw a rose tattooed above her left breast and a flying dragon on the back of her right shoulder. She was relaxed and affectionate now, unworried and unreserved.

In the morning she fixed coffee, and they sat cater-cornered at the small kitchen table. Rory asked if she expected her ex to come by any time soon, and she said, no, not until

Sunday afternoon. She had time to get her house picked up in the meanwhile.

She asked what he was going to do today, and he said he was going to get a few things together, to be ready to go hunting next weekend.

"By the way," he said, "I don't know if Danny mentioned it, but the day I met him, he gave me a gun to keep for him."

She raised her eyebrows, then shook her head. "He didn't say anything about it. What kind of gun?"

"It's a little deer rifle. Called a .30-30, if you know what that is."

She shook her head again.

"I saw him a couple of times after that, just passing by, but I didn't get a chance to talk to him. And I'm kind of wonderin' now what I should do with the gun."

"Did he say it was his?"

"He said he got it in a deal."

"He probably did, then."

"Do you have any use for it?"

"Oh, no."

"Any idea of what I should do with it?"

She narrowed her eyes as she gazed at her coffee cup. Then she looked at Rory. "Just keep it. You were his friend. You helped him out. He'd want you to have it."

* * * * *

When Rory went hunting on opening morning, he put the .30-30 in the gun rack even though he didn't expect to use it. The

.270 had a scope, and it shot so much flatter and farther that there was no comparison. Still, with one antelope and two deer permits, he thought he might find a moment to try the smaller rifle.

In the middle of the first morning, he was driving west through the rolling grassland on a ranch where he had permission. Off to his right, he saw a small herd down in a swale by a windmill. It looked like a band he had seen earlier, a group that did not let him get near. So he parked the pickup in a low spot, got out the .270, and started walking up the slope that kept him and the antelope out of each other's view. The sun was also at his back, so he counted that as an advantage.

Partway up the hill, he took off his wool jacket to use as a cushion for his aim. On the crest of the slope he saw a flat rock, maybe sixteen inches wide and four inches high. Crab-walking, then crawling on all fours, and then crawling on his stomach, he finally got to the crest and looked at the antelope. There were six of them in the morning light, all of them about four hundred yards away—a long shot but the best one he was likely to get that morning. He laid his jacket on the rock to get a good steady rest. Then he scoped the animals, first one and then another, seeing which would give him a good profile and which was best for his position. He decided that the one on his left, although it wasn't the biggest, was the most feasible shot. He bore down and focused on his aim. When everything came together and he thought he had his best shot, he fired.

The antelope ran forward, stopped, ran a little further, and then flopped. Rory's heart lifted. It was the best shot he had made on an antelope in several years, and it felt even better for being part of a slow, careful sneak.

He waited to make sure the animal wasn't going to get up again; then he walked down the hill to the pickup to put away his rifle and get out the tow rope. When he opened the door of the cab, he saw the .30-30 in the rack. He shrugged. He would never have made a shot like that with the little brush gun.

Later the next day, on the same ranch, he was hunting in the breaks for deer. A cool breeze had come up, so he put on his jacket and set out on foot. When he hunted in the afternoon, he worked from the west, again with the sun at his back. He walked along through the grass, up and down draws, and along the rocks. He climbed a slope on the west side of some rocks where he had shot a nice deer two years earlier, in a little valley between two bluffs. As he eased up toward the crest, he glanced off toward the south where he had seen a couple of antlerless deer the year before.

In the shadow of the bluff he saw the dark silhouette of a deer head sticking up above the dry grass. It looked as if it had antlers. Rory ducked out of sight, eased a shell into the chamber, and came back up with some rocks as cover. He put the scope on the deer and saw that it didn't have big antlers but it was a buck. Rory crept along the base of the rocks, with the bluff rising on his right. Although the deer did not show any more than his head and neck, he did turn a couple of times, and the antlers were evident. Rory got a good steady rest on a rock, but he did not feel good about the shot. It was somewhere in the range of two hundred yards, and all he had was the head and neck to shoot at. He sat for several minutes, changed position, changed back, and still had no change. Then the deer stood up, and Rory narrowed in on a shot.

A chip of rock flew up in the air, and the shot did not hit the deer. He stood there in profile and turned his head each way. Rory moved to another rock for a clearer shot, and he fired again. He thought he hit the deer, but he wasn't sure. He jacked in another shell, made himself bear down even more than before, and fired again. This time the animal lurched, bolted forward, ran down the hillside, and tumbled.

Rory felt a lift in his spirits as he walked down the slope. He had his deer, and on opening weekend, along with his antelope. As he stood over the still form, he checked his watch. It was 5:10 p.m., and the shadows were stretching. He figured he had time to go get the pickup and drive down in here, where he could use the hoist on the vehicle to skin the animal. The cooling air would be good for the carcass, and the solitude would be enjoyable.

When he reached the pickup and opened the door of the cab, he saw the .30-30 again. For a moment he had to consider whether the gun had brought him good luck, just from being along for the ride. He couldn't decide. He believed in luck, some kinds, but he would have to think about this one.

* * * * *

A week later, he went out to try to fill his second deer permit, which was doe or fawn only. Now he was meat-hunting, pure and simple. Having gotten permission south of town, he was out in the farm country at sunup. Right away he saw some deer at the edge of a cornfield, but when he got the pickup parked and went back on foot, the deer had gone into hiding. He hunted through the morning, taking long walks around hayfields and along the ends of corn rows. Things slowed down at midday, and then when the shadows started to stretch to the east, he started the rounds again.

Close to dusk, he parked the pickup near where he had first seen deer that morning. On a whim, he decided to try the .30-30, so he pulled it from the rack and crept along the edge of the cornfield. When he came to the corner where the corn rows met an alfalfa field, he got down on all fours, crawled forward, and took a peek. A small bunch of deer, most of them with heads down and grazing, stood in the shadows on the edge of the alfalfa. Rory settled back and levered a shell into the chamber, slow and quiet. Then he stood up, and in a split second he had to determine which animals had no horns, that the best prospect was a large doe that had not yet bolted, and that it was in the clear. He shot the deer offhand, at a not-very-great distance of fifty or sixty yards. It raised up on its hind legs, showing its dark chest, and then it fell over. One shot. Not bad.

The rest of the bunch had disappeared. Rory made sure of his kill and then went for his equipment. For a few minutes, as he walked along, he felt as if all he had done was shoot a doe at the edge of a cornfield; but as he mulled it over, he decided that it had taken some skill in the stalking as well as a good shot. Then, as he poked the carbine into the rack, he considered that he might have had a little luck as well.

Rory concentrated on doing a neat job of dressing the animal. The deer was a good fat one, nothing to apologize for if a fellow was meat-hunting. He reminded himself that the Game and Fish wouldn't sell the permits, and the farmer wouldn't be so agreeable, if the herds weren't up. And the gun worked out fine, too. He hadn't known what to think of it before, but now he had brought it into the category it was supposed to be in.

Maybe Shawna was right, that Danny would have wanted him to have it. There was nothing wrong with that idea, either.

Rory straightened his back and rested for a moment. This deer would have a lot of good steaks on it. Between the jerky and the sausage and the table meat, he could make use of all the animals he hunted. But it seemed as if the balance would come out better if he took a few packages of this one to Shawna.

Drunk on Christmas Day

The bus hit a deer in the night. At first it was just a deep thump against metal, followed by a drop in the bus's speed. I had been drowsing off, as I imagine most of the other passengers had been doing, but after the impact there was a bustle and hubbub as people sat up in their seats, cleared their throats, coughed, and asked one another what the noise was. Word came back from the driver, a woman, that it was a deer. As she brought the bus to a long, slow stop along the edge of the highway, one of the passengers was laughing as he repeated the news.

A couple of reading lights came on as the driver put on a coat and went out to look things over. The deer would be quite a ways back, I thought, and not of much consequence to the driver. I felt sorry for the deer, and I always hated to see one go to waste, but I was glad the driver had taken her time to slow down on the snowy highway.

If it hadn't been for the road conditions, I wouldn't have taken the bus. I would have driven. If it hadn't been for my brother's condition, I wouldn't have gone anywhere until the weather got better, but his girlfriend said he was bloated up and in the hospital. I knew all too well what that meant—I had seen it in our father, at the same age—and I had the general sense that a person who got to that stage might come out of the hospital the first time but not the second. So I made arrangements to take a few days off work. After checking road conditions, weather forecasts, air fares, and bus schedules, all in a medley of phone calls and internet searches, I drove to Casper and took the long bus ride to Billings and Bozeman. Now I was on the way back. I told myself there was no such thing as a hurry when a fellow traveled like this; he would get there when he got there. And besides, I had plenty to think about.

My brother was back home, in the dim light of his living room, smoking cigarettes and sipping on a beer, when I left. I had gotten there in time to help drive him home from the hospital and then to see how daunted he was by it all. The two of them took it slow—getting up out of a chair, shuffling to the refrigerator, sinking back into the chair, lighting a cigarette, switching the channels on the t.v. Even the invitation to stay over for Christmas came out as something incidental, along with a comment that some friends were coming over.

I said I thought I had better start back, as it had been a long trip up and there was no telling how long it would take for the return. That much was the truth. The part I left out was my reluctance to spend Christmas Day with drunks.

I had done it before, at their place, when they lived in Cheyenne. I had driven down early in the day, thinking I would sit around sipping coffee as the turkey cooked and then join in on the drinking when the meal hit the table. But when I got to their place, the only person at home was a bleary-eyed, pasty-faced guy in his forties who said everyone else had gone to get Bev out of jail. He spoke in weeping tones, as if it had been one of those tragedies that struck without mercy.

"And on Christmas," he said.

I asked what she had done to get thrown in, and he told me she had hit another car in the parking lot at Scooter's. Now Larry and a couple of their friends were trying to get her out. I asked the guy if he was a friend of Bev's, or Larry's, or both, which was my way of asking what he was doing at their place when no one else was at home, and he told me he was her brother. I looked at him and didn't see any resemblance, and he must have understood my look, because he went on to explain that they had adopted one another. Great, I thought—the fabled love of one drunk for another, complete with pity.

After a few hours of sitting in a kitchenette cabin with this moping spiritual brother, I heard a pickup come to a stop outside, and in came Larry and Bev with a case of beer and a tall, overweight fellow. They went through the story as they brought out some potato chips, opened a can of olives, and decided it was too late to cook the turkey. They dug out a canned ham and put slices of it to heat in the microwave as Bev cooked some instant mashed potatoes on the stove top. All the time they talked about what a bum deal it was to get thrown in the can, what jerks the cops were, and this was Christmas, by God. I drank four beers with them and ate my ham and mashed potatoes, all in the stale atmosphere of people who had been up all night smoking and drinking and dealing with the law.

I was no stranger to drinking myself, and I had even drunk a couple of cheap beers with my brother before I caught the bus out of Bozeman. I just didn't want to go through a repeat of the squalor I had sat through that day in Cheyenne. So here

I was on the bus, somewhere out on the highway between Bozeman and Billings, with snow falling in the headlights, the diesel engine idling, and a few passengers making small talk while a deer lay dead or crippled on the roadside half a mile back.

The bus I was riding would go northeast toward Miles City, so I was getting off in Billings. I planned to stay over and catch a bus to Sheridan and Casper the next day. I got off the bus downtown at a little after midnight—about an hour and a half later than expected—and walked out into the cold, carrying a bag in each hand and hoping the exercise would help me work up some warmth.

It was quiet and lonely and cold as a bitch, down near zero from the feel of it, with light snow falling and a few inches of it to walk through. I could feel the cold come right through my coat, so I walked fast. The first motel I came to wanted eighty dollars for a room, but the desk clerk was a sympathetic young woman and she told me of a less expensive place a few blocks away. So I pushed back out into the cold and found my way to the Westerner, where in a little while I was lodged in a tolerable room. In the short time I had been on the street, I felt as if I had been set down in a frigid, impersonal place, far from anyone or anything I knew. Now I had a warm room, with drapes and carpet and blankets, a thermostat, hot running water, coffee for the morning, and a t.v. for the weather report. I might be a long ways from everything, but I was going to sleep all right.

In the morning I called the bus station and found out that the road was closed farther south. Even if the roads opened later in the day, the earliest bus I would be able to take out of Billings would be at seven in the evening. That would mean another night on the bus, on icy roads. I decided to go have breakfast and think about how I was going to do things.

I ordered steak and eggs, and what I thought about, in addition to what a thin, tough steak I had gotten, was what a crummy holiday Christmas could be. Not that I minded spending it alone in a place where I didn't know anyone—quite to the contrary, I thought it wasn't a bad way to get through the day.

Larry and I had been through more than one miserable Christmas. Either our father ruined the whole thing by getting drunk and throwing a fit, or we picked through second-hand toys donated by some charity. I didn't like soldiers and tanks, and when I got them, I understood that it was through someone's vague notion of what Christmas was supposed to consist of—canned goods for a poor family, all-purpose toys for young, poor boys. After the dreary, washed-out feeling of having to receive gifts I never wanted and that no one picked out for me, I had to go to school and listen to the other kids talk about what they had gotten.

In private I learned to hate Christmas, especially the gift-giving part of it, when so many people bought presents because they thought they had to and the commercial force of America pushed on a person to hope for something he would never get and then to hope he got nothing because he would like it better. Once when we were in our twenties, Larry and I went out and got drunk on Christmas Eve, then went back to his place and slept in till noon. When we got up I said to him,

"Good. We got rid of the first half of this son of a bitch. Let's see what we can do about the second half." If the old man hadn't called us and asked us to please come over after all, we would have gotten away clean.

Back in my room at the Westerner, I called the station again and found out there was still nothing certain about the evening bus. With checkout time at eleven, I decided to stay where I was and hope for the 8:05 departure the next morning. That would be all right. At least I knew where I was and what I was doing. And it wasn't the first time I was snowbound in a cheap hotel.

I went across the parking lot to the office and paid for another night's stay, then beat it back to the room. The day wasn't warming up at all. It was grey and drab, and according to the t.v., the temperature was staying at ten degrees. I flipped through the channels, skipping the jingle bells and Santa Claus scenes as fast as I could. I came to a movie about a family of dirt farmers waiting to see if the flood waters were going to reach their place. I watched it for a little while and then shut off the set.

It was barely eleven o'clock, and I was beginning to wonder how I was going to fill up the day. As I sat in the armchair, I spent a little time glancing around the room, appreciating the western decor. The closet door and the bathroom door were both made of pine, dark-stained boards held together with cross-X's and set off with black iron hinges and latches. From where I sat I could see into the bathroom and observe the tile work I had seen before but hadn't noticed. It was colorful old tile, mostly of a turquoise hue, with a square now and then that had an illustration in pink and dark brown of a cowboy sitting with his hat in his lap, one leg bent and one leg straight out, as his horse ran arching away.

After I had confirmed the layout of the cowboy tiles (every sixth one, going across, and staggered every third row, up and down), and after I had verified that he was in the same posture in every one, I let my mind drift. I got to thinking about the flood waters in the movie, and I remembered a time when we were living on a farm where our father worked. The river was rising by inches and inches, and volunteers were going out to stack sandbags on the levee. Our old man didn't go. Instead, he put a ladder in the bathroom, where there was a crawl-hole to the attic, and he put a hatchet on the top step of the ladder. Nothing came of it. We evacuated the house for one night when the river reached its highest, but the levee didn't break, and we never had to find out how hard it would be to chop our way out onto the roof.

I shook off that memory and realized I needed to find something to do. I had already read the magazines I had brought along for the bus ride, and I thought I might be able to find a supermarket or convenience store where I could find something to read. I was in the mood for a nice, cheery story about an ax murderer who struck on Christmas Day, but I thought I could get by with an average murder mystery. That was what I told myself, anyway. But I had also been thinking about things I had read and heard about Christmas being a peak time for depression and suicide, and even though I didn't think I was susceptible, I wanted to get out of that room. So I put on my hat and coat and walked out into the numb day.

Once I was away from Room 137, I started feeling better. I was in a big town where I didn't know anybody and I didn't have any obligations. My room was paid for, whenever I felt like going back. In the meanwhile I could walk along the empty streets, ignore the Christmas decorations, and be glad I wasn't stuck somewhere worse.

I walked a few blocks in one direction and a few blocks in another, not worrying about how soon I would find a supermarket. I was still downtown, walking past jewelry stores, travel agencies, western wear shops, and bookstores—all closed. A couple of hotel lobbies were lit up, and a dingy little greasy-spoon restaurant had light glowing behind the tinseled windows. Then I found something that I may or may not have been looking for. It was called the Pastime, and I could hear human voices inside. Among them I heard a woman's voice, then the slap of a dice cup and the rattle of ivory on a bar top.

With a clear sense that it was not yet noon, I pushed on the door and walked into the dim saloon. A thin bald man stood behind the bar, and three patrons sat on stools. All four people looked at me as I walked in. I took a seat at the end of the bar, nodded at the other customers, and ordered a glass of tomato juice. The bartender brought me a tall glass with an asparagus spear sticking up from the drink. I put a ten on the bar and took a slow look around.

Everything seemed to be settled into its place in the Pastime. The bartender had his stool next to the cash register, and the three drinkers in front of him had the easy slouch and calm chatter of regulars. A woman with a puffy face and frizzled blonde hair sat between a clean-shaven, jowly fellow and a dark-haired, dark-eyed man with a salt-and-pepper beard. They all had mixed drinks, change, and cigarettes in front of them, and they looked as if they could handle a long siege. As my eyes got adjusted and I took in the rest of the place, I saw a black-and-white enamel roasting oven on a service table, along with stacks of napkins, plastic plates, and styrofoam bowls. A little orange light glowed from the controls of the roaster, and I picked up a trace of cooked turkey floating on the air along with the tobacco smoke and liquor fumes.

The man with the jowls said, "Let's finish rollin' for the music."

The bartender got up from his stool and took turns thumping the leather cup on the bar. Then he reached into a glass by the cash register, drew out four quarters, and handed them to the woman, who walked to the far wall and fed the coins into the juke box. I told myself that if she played some pukey Santa Claus or Frosty the Snowman song I would walk out of there, but things got much better than that. She played "Blue Christmas" by Ernest Tubb.

If a fellow has to listen to Christmas songs, that's the kind to hear—something full of heartache and loneliness, well rhymed and droned out, to stay on top of the real misery. The guy in the song tells it straight, that he'll have a blue Christmas without her, that the red decorations on a green tree won't mean a thing, that she can enjoy her white Christmas but his will be blue. As I listened to the song, I appreciated the restraint. I didn't hear anything in it that would make a person feel sorry for himself, just the matter-of-fact statement, not too sharp on the edges, that not everybody had it warm and happy.

The song played through, as did some others that I didn't listen to. I had drawn into myself, thinking that this was not the worst way of getting rid of part of the day. I finished the tomato juice and ordered a beer, and before long the jukebox was playing the Ernest Tubb song again. Now I was in the flow, nodding to the melody of a blue heartache, not drinking too fast, hearing the slam of the dice cup and the pitter-patter of small talk.

I drank a second beer, still minding my own business. When I ordered my third one, the bartender sat two in front of me. I gave him a questioning look.

"Happy hour is at one today."

"Oh. Thanks." I looked down the bar and saw that the other three customers had drinks stacked in front of them as well.

The woman saw me looking, so I waved at her. A couple of minutes later I heard her voice.

"Hey, you at the end of the bar. What's your name?"

"Bernie."

"Merry Christmas, Bernie."

"Thanks. Same to you."

The man in the salt-and-pepper beard, who sat closer to me, raised his glass and said, "Yeah. Merry Christmas."

"What's your name?" I called to her.

"Carol. And this here's Lannie." Then, pointing to her left at the man with the jowls, she said, "And this is Ed."

I nodded to all of them.

Carol lit a cigarette. "We're gonna have turkey dinner in a little while, so don't leave too soon. Isn't that right, Tinker?"

The bartender nodded and brought his cigarette up to his lips.

It was the fourth beer that got me stuck in that place. I can walk out after two beers, and maybe even three, but if I've had four and I've got nothing else to do, and especially if I don't have to drive, I'm not likely to pull up and leave. So I sat through the middle part of the afternoon, drinking beer, eating a few slices of turkey, listening to "Blue Christmas" now and again, and telling myself that even if I was spending Christmas Day with a group of drunks after all, at least I could get up and walk out if I wanted.

I stayed in that flow until I'd had about six beers, I think. Then the atmosphere changed. A couple of other people had come in for one or two drinks and left, but the main group consisted of the other three, Tinker, and me, until a red-faced guy with bulging eyes came in. He looked like he was in his early forties and trying to preserve some earlier version of being hip, with long blond hair tucked behind his ears and a gold chain around his neck. The others all said "Hi" to him, but he didn't fall into their group. He looked as if he was wound up about something, and I noticed him shaking as he took out his wallet. When the others asked him what the hell was wrong, he blurted out that he had heard Randy had gotten killed in a car wreck.

Silence fell on the place for a long moment until Tinker shook his head and spoke. "Not Randy."

"I can't believe it," Lannie said. "He was just in here last night."

Tinker set a bottle of Budweiser on the bar. "Are you sure of this, Sticks?"

The red-faced guy took in a deep breath and pushed it out through his nose, keeping his jaw clenched, until he said, "I just heard it at the Rendezvous. You can call over there if you want."

Tinker frowned. "Nah. If you just heard it there, I wouldn't find out anything different."

Carol was shaking her head and biting her lip, and her eyes were brimming with tears. "It's not fair," she said. "Not on Christmas."

Sticks unzipped his parka, shook out a cigarette, and lit it. Then he took a drink of his beer and gazed at the television above the back of the bar, where a football game was playing in silence. He was standing between me and the other three customers, and as I observed him, I couldn't help thinking that he felt important at being the one to bear the news. I also thought he looked a little absurd in his agony. Beyond him, the other three were talking among themselves.

Then Ed spoke up in what sounded like a bossy voice. "Well, what about Randy? Was he driving? Or was he with someone? Did it happen today? Or last night?"

Sticks shook his head. "I don't know any details. I just heard that it happened earlier today."

The other three fell back into their conversation, saying again in one way or another how terrible it was, especially on Christmas. I had the sense that Sticks felt left out of their family council, or that he felt he had at least an equal claim on what happened to Randy. Every twenty or thirty seconds, he turned his head toward them, and finally he responded to something that one of them said.

"That doesn't make it anything special in itself. Billy Martin died on Christmas Day, in a car wreck."

I heard Carol say something that sounded like, "Was he drunk?"

Sticks tossed back an answer. "Oh, he was a hell of a drunk."

"No," said Lannie. "What she means is, was he drunk when he died?"

"I think so. They don't really know if he was driving, but he'd been drinking, like you could expect of him, especially on a holiday. It was an icy road, I remember that. I was in the Rendezvous when it came on the news. Gotta be more than ten years ago now."

"No!" Carol shouted. "I'm not asking about Billy Martin, for Christ's sake! I'm asking about Randy. What happened to him?"

Sticks had an impatient tone to his voice, and he only halfway looked away from the football game. "I don't know. All I heard was he got killed in a wreck."

"You don't seem to care much," Lannie said.

Sticks took a deep quivering breath. "Randy was as good a friend of mine as he was to any of you."

Tinker slammed an empty drink glass on the bar. Everyone looked at him as he said, "Jesus Christ! Are we gonna argue about who cares the most?"

Lannie spoke with an air of calmness. “Until we know more, I think we should just remember Randy as we knew him the best.”

Ed’s voice came up from the other side of the group. “That’s right. There’s nothing we can do to change anything.”

Sticks lifted his chin and squared his shoulders, in an attitude of authority. “Fuck it. Let’s drink a shot. On me. Go ahead, Tinker. Set ’em up. This is for Randy.”

Tinker looked my way.

“None for me,” I said. “I can’t drink shots.”

Lannie said he would, but Ed shook his head.

“I’ll drink one,” Carol said.

Tinker poured four shots of apple schnapps and lifted his as the others did.

“Here’s to Randy,” said Sticks. “He was like a brother to all of us.”

“He was a good fuckin’ guy,” said Carol.

I heard a quaver in her voice. I realized she had been drinking since before I came in, and I imagined her brave talk was a way of trying to brace herself up.

“Amen,” Lannie added. And the four shots went down the hatch.

Sticks made a smacking sound with his lips. “Sumbitch. That went down too easy. I think I could drink another one. Anyone else? I’ll pay for ’em all together.”

Tinker shook his head and looked at the other two. Lannie said, “Not yet,” and Carol said, “No.” Then she said, “How about you, Bernie?”

“No, thanks.”

"If you have one, I will."

The only reason I would have had a shot at that point would have been that I thought it would help me get a woman back to my room at the Westerner, but Carol was so stuck in place between Lannie and Ed, and so far away from the kind of woman I might usually hope for, that I was able to resist.

"No, thanks," I said. "I'd better not."

"Fuck it," she said to Tinker. "I'll have one anyway."

Sticks seemed happy at that, and in another minute he had downed his shot and chased it with a good slug of beer. Then he looked at Carol's shot glass, which still sat full on the bar. "What's the matter?"

"I had a hard time swallowin' for a minute there."

"You ought to practice more."

"What?"

"Nothin'."

"Well, fuck you, Sticks. I heard what you said. I don't want your fuckin' drink."

"Ah, c'mon, Carol."

"Nah, fuck you."

"What's wrong?"

"There's nothin' wrong with me. But you've had somethin' in your ass ever since you came in here. And now you're tryin' to start shit."

"I'm not tryin' to start any shit."

She waved her hand. "Well, I'm not gonna drink that shot."

"Fine. I'll drink it." He peeled out a twenty and flipped it onto the bar, then motioned for the drink. Lannie pushed it down the bar to him as Tinker picked up the twenty with two fingers and moved away. Sticks took another drink of beer, looked at his bottle, and said, "I'll have another Bud while you're at it."

Tinker brought the beer and set it down with the change. Sticks left the two quarters on the bar but put the dollar bills in his wallet.

He was getting all his drinks positioned in front of him when another fellow walked in. The guy stood between me and Sticks and held up one finger. The others all said, "Hi, Frank," and Tinker set down a bottle of Schlitz. Frank pinched out three dollars and took a drink of his beer.

He was a slender type, with his pants tucked into his boots. He wore a denim coat with fake sheepskin lining, an old striped western shirt with a pack of cigarettes in each pocket, and a high-necked t-shirt beneath that. He had long sideburns and a head of dark, wavy hair combed back on the sides and over on top. He smiled out of the right side of his mouth, and his face had a little twitch to it. I would guess he was the oldest one in the bar, and I wouldn't have put a lot of money on his making it to sixty.

Sticks moved his drinks to the left, to make more room. "What do you know, Frank?"

"Nothin'. Never did."

"Me neither." Sticks shook his head. "We were just talkin' about Randy. Did you hear about it?"

Frank tipped up his bottle for a drink and then set it down on the bar. "Ah, that was just a bunch of shit."

"What do you mean?"

"There's nothin' wrong with Randy. I just saw him in the Rendezvous."

"The hell you did."

"The hell I didn't. He came in right after you left. Go see for yourself."

Lannie spoke up. "So he's all right, then?"

"Gittin' drunk as an Indian, and wonderin' why people are spreadin' rumors, but he's all in one piece."

"Well, I'll be damned." Sticks picked up the shot glass and downed the schnapps.

"He's a little pissed, I'll tell you that."

"What for? You'd think he'd be glad to be alive."

"Well, he was drunk when he got there, and he thought someone was makin' light of him."

"It wasn't me. I don't remember who said it first, but I heard it in there."

Carol's voice came out, with a whining edge to it. "Yeah, but then you come in here talkin' shit, and you get everyone worked up for nothin'."

"Oh, shut up, Carol."

"You and your big mouth. Just talkin' shit."

"Oh, shut up."

"Makin' light of him, just like he said. What if someone went around and talked shit about you?"

"For all I know, they do."

"You wish. Even if they did, you wouldn't find many people who gave a shit."

Sticks yelled something like "Aa-agh!" as he flung his beer bottle. Tinker had taken the empty shot glass away, so

Sticks had an open field to send the almost empty bottle sliding down the bar and crashing into the colony of mixed drinks. Carol screamed, Lannie and Ed pushed back from the bar swearing, and Tinker came up and around with a pistol pointed at Sticks.

It was a little .38, just like the one I used to wear in a shoulder holster when I worked in an all-night gas station in Rawlins. That was over twenty years ago, but I'd know the model anywhere, with its small handle and short barrel.

Tinker held the gun steady with his right hand as he reached across with his left and brought out a cordless phone.

"Just get out of here. You don't pull that kind of shit when I'm behind the bar."

"I'm sorry. I don't know why I did it. I guess things just stacked up on me."

"Yeah," Carol said. "Like three shots in five minutes."

"Just get out," Tinker said. "Or I'm callin' the cops."

Sticks lifted his hand toward the bar. "Can I drink my beer?"

"Get the fuck out. If you so much as touch that bottle, I'll have to stop you. So just leave."

"Fine." Sticks put up his hands. "Throw me out on the street on Christmas Day. Like Carol says, no one gives a shit about me anyway." He turned and moved toward the door, and I made a point of not watching him. I tried not to watch Tinker as well, so I didn't see where the .38 went. But I did notice it disappeared.

Not long after Sticks walked out, I heard something like a *thunk*, then a sliding, rasping sound and the crunch of metal on metal. It sounded as if a car had hit something and then slid into another car. Within a minute there came the sound of voices, a horn honking, and car doors slamming. A couple of minutes later, I heard the sirens. Those of us in the bar looked at each other, and Frank said he would go find out what happened.

As he opened the door, I could see it was dark outside, and I remembered that in the dead of winter it gets dark even earlier in Montana than it does in Wyoming.

Frank wasn't gone long, and he came back in shivering. "It looks like Sticks got hit by a car," he said, twisting the same side of his mouth that he had smiled out of earlier.

Nobody spoke for a few seconds, until Tinker said, "I hope he's not hurt too bad."

Frank shrugged. "I don't know."

I had half a beer left and was in no hurry to go out into the cold air, vehicle fumes, and flashing lights, so I just sat on my stool and kept to myself. In a little while, a cop came into the bar. He was wearing a thick coat and carrying a flashlight. He stopped a few feet from the rail and looked at Tinker.

"A pedestrian got hit by a car out front here. He's got long blond hair and is wearing a blue-and-yellow winter coat. He has the appearance of having had a lot to drink, so I thought I would ask in here if you'd seen him."

Tinker nodded with a thoughtful expression. "A fella by that description left here just before the commotion started. How did he get hit?"

"It's not clear. The driver of the car says he didn't see him until he stepped out into the headlights."

I wondered if it was self-pity or the three shots in five minutes, or some combination.

Tinker just shook his head.

The cop looked to either side and then back at Tinker. "Like I said, he seems to have had a lot to drink."

"He wasn't in here very long, but no tellin' how much he had to drink before that."

"Did he get over-served in here?"

Tinker pushed out his lips and moved his head back and forth. "He wasn't in here that long, and I even took his last drink from him because I didn't like the way he was acting."

"Did you know him?"

"Oh, yeah. He goes by Sticks."

"Was he a regular in here?"

I noticed the cop was speaking of him in the past tense now.

"I guess you could say that."

"Do you know if he had anything personal working on him?"

"Lots of people who come in here do."

"You don't know of anything that might have set him off, though? Like losing his job or having a wife leave him? People take those things hard at this time of the year."

Tinker lit a cigarette. "Don't know of anything. He didn't talk much about his problems." Then, as he snapped his lighter shut, he said, "Is he hurt very bad?"

"He might be."

I walked back to the Westerner when I finished my beer. I had a pretty good buzz going, but I was able to walk straight and keep an eye out for traffic. Later that night, on the local news, I learned that two people had died in traffic accidents that day "to mar the holiday happiness." Early in the day, a man named Randy something-or-other from Great Falls had slid his car off an on-ramp and rolled it several times. In the late afternoon, a pedestrian named Garret Richards had been struck down by a car in the downtown area. Without looking straight at the camera, the newsman added that "police cited alcohol as a factor in both accidents that brought tragedy to Christmas Day."

I imagine sometimes people say things like that as flat as they can so the public won't think they're preaching, but it doesn't save the flatness from sounding stupid. Not that I didn't feel stupid myself for being a part of it all, but I knew a lot of people had gotten drunk separately that day—not least among them my brother, myself, the man from Great Falls, Sticks, and the other Randy who didn't die after all—and I imagined that behind every one of them was a story that wouldn't get told in full.

Dusk on the Rangeland

The pickup tires thumped across the cattle guard as Brad drove into the lane that led to the ranch house. Off to his left, just visible in first daylight, sat the various hulks of old cars, pickups, tractors, spray rigs, and the like. Straight ahead, an old Ford flatbed truck was backed halfway into a metal shed. Turning right into the yard, he saw that the barnyard life had already begun to stir. The place looked very much as he remembered it—maybe a little junkier, but probably no more so than it had really been.

He recalled the first time he had been on the ranch, a year earlier. It started with the two men he met out on the road. One was wearing a winter cap with ear lugs, while the other was wearing a felt cowboy hat. The man with the cap was driving a Chevy pickup with dual rear wheels; with the help of a tow chain gummed up with mud, he was pulling a red International pickup hooked to a stock trailer. The dually had plates from Niobrara County, which lay on the north side of the road, while the International and the trailer had plates from Goshen County, which was on the south side.

The men told Brad they had land on either side and he could hunt wherever his permits were good. He told them he had one permit for Area 13, which was Goshen County. They told him he could hunt and if he got an antelope he should give the landowner coupon to the old man. The old man, whose name turned out to be Duncan, had been standing off to the side of the road, watching the other two men in their pickups trying to pull the trailer full of cattle out of the gumbo.

Brad remembered the old man, not very tall, with watery eyes and a seedy, unkempt aspect. He had been friendly and talkative enough when Brad came back through in the afternoon. Like most landholders, the old man didn't show any interest in seeing the animal itself. He just took the coupon and chatted awhile about the weather and how the antelope came and went and you never knew if there were any out there.

As a general rule, Brad asked fewer questions than the ranch folk did, so he didn't know if one or even both of the men in the pickups were Duncan's sons. But if the old man collected the landowner coupons, he probably had the authority to give permission to hunt, so Brad had come straight to the ranch house to ask this time. He switched off the pickup lights and killed the engine. He expected a dog to materialize, barking, out of the morning shapes, or a cat to come arching out of the shadows, but only the ducks and the geese and the guinea hens stirred, moving to either side as he walked to the door.

After rapping twice on the wooden door frame, he heard hollering from the inside. Thinking that he was being invited in, he opened the door and called out a greeting.

A rugged voice told him to come on in.

He followed the voice to the living room, where the old man lay beneath a heap of blankets on a narrow bed. Morning light came through an unshaded window on the east. Brad could see the other shapes in the room as well—an old couch, a stack of newspapers, a television on a flimsy wheeled cart.

"Good morning, Mr. Duncan."

"And the same to you."

"My name's Brad Westley. I hunted out here on your place last year, and I was wondering if it might be all right to give it another try this year."

"Where do you have your tags for?"

"Area 13, on the south side of the road here."

The old man was quiet for a couple of seconds until he said, "Yeah, that should be all right." He cleared his throat. "You say you hunted out here last year?"

"Uh-huh. I gave you the landowner coupon for one antelope."

"Oh, uh-huh. Well, it should be all right. You know your way around, then."

"I'll remember when I see it." Brad paused. "Is there anything I can do for you?"

"Oh, no. I'm fine. I'm just in no hurry to get up when the weather starts gettin' cold."

Brad nodded. "I suppose I'll go ahead, then. I appreciate it."

"You bet. Just follow the windmills, you know. That's the best way."

"It seems to be. I'll stay on the roads."

"That's good. I don't know how many's out there, but you should find one."

Brad thanked the old man again and walked out, closing the door behind him. The sun was coming up now, and the shapes around the ranch yard were more visible. It would be time for the antelope to be moving around; they didn't get up as early as the deer did.

He drove out between two rows of hulk vehicles and implements, then angled southwest along a dirt path. When he came to a gate he got out, opened the gate, drove through, closed the gate, and drove on. The two big rules of cow country—close any gates you open, and stay on the roads unless you have to pick up an animal—were easy enough. He followed the road until he came within a quarter of a mile of the first windmill.

He stopped and shut off the engine, partly to keep himself from being in a hurry, and partly to keep his elbows from vibrating as he leaned on the window sill and steering wheel to look through the binoculars. Nothing moved. He saw the windmill, the tank, the shadowy worked-up ground where the mud had dried, and the pale grass that sloped up and away.

Satisfied that there were no cattle or antelope, he fired up the engine and drove past the windmill, then followed the road nearly straight south. He rumbled along for half a mile until he came to a corner gate, not far from the next windmill. He shut off the engine again, remembering that this was the place where he had killed an antelope the year before.

The song of a meadowlark fluted on the morning air as he sneaked from the pickup to the fence brace. He settled the rifle against a post and scoped the windmill. Again there was nothing—no cattle, no antelope, not even a rabbit. He was disappointed in a familiar way. If a fellow saw an animal in a certain spot, he always expected to see one there again.

The windmill was turning in the light breeze, sending a creak out onto the cold air. The lark sang again, and the windmill creaked a tune. Brad thought that if he waited a few minutes an antelope might appear, so he hunkered down. As he knelt there, crouched, vacating his mind to the sound of the windmill, he began to hear a song.

> She used to call me darlin'
> Now she don't call me any more.

He didn't know if he had ever really heard the song before, but he heard it now.

He waited for several minutes, then stood up and scoped the area again. He decided to walk to the windmill. After checking to be sure he hadn't slipped a shell into the chamber, he crawled between the barbed-wire strands. The meadowlark had quit singing, but the windmill kept up its tune.

As he moved closer to the windmill, he saw hundreds of sunken hoofprints left by loitering cattle. Away from the tank in the sunlit area, all the frost was gone, even in the dark of the hoof-pocks, but in the solid shadow of the tank, frost lay on the ground.

The frost brought back a memory of another ranch, in a year gone by. On a morning like this one, chilly at first light, he had shot an antelope and dragged it back to the pickup. There he had skinned it on the ground, turning it from one side to the other, as the morning warmed and the meadowlarks sang. That was before he had his hunter's helper, the frame and hoist that allowed him to hang an animal and skin it, out on the treeless prairie. It had been a morning to remember, calm and peaceful, as he went about his work and took satisfaction in doing it well. The dragging and the skinning had kept him warm in the rising sun, but when he had finished, frost still lay on the grass on the shady side of the pickup.

Now at the windmill, he took note of its layout. The frame was all lumber, old and weathered, with four-by-four legs bolted a foot or so off the ground to four heavier posts sunk into the ground. Brad wondered if this windmill had replaced an earlier one, as he could see the top piece of a windmill—tail, blades, and motor—lying face down in the sand and weeds on the other side of the current structure. Looking up, he could see that this windmill was not new even though it was intact and working. The blades were spinning in the light breeze, and the tail was peppered with dark holes—probably .22 shots. Looking down from the head of the windmill, he saw the gear housing, then a rod that moved slowly up and down inside an inch-and-a-half pipe, which passed through the cement slab that served as a cap or base. Coming off the upright at a tee, a horizontal pipe delivered water to the tank. The water came out in spills of about half a cup at a time.

The tank had an old barbed-wire fence on three sides of it, plus corrugated tin covering three-fourths of the top. Cattle—or antelope—could drink from only one side and would be less likely to climb in. Once, years earlier, he had seen an antelope plunge into a water tank, but that had been unusual. Brad's hunting pal Darin had shot the antelope as it looked up and around from taking a drink, and it leaped forward. Even in those circumstances, a cover such as this one might have kept the animal out.

Looking down into the clear water, Brad could see the bottom of the tank, which was strewn with the remains of dead birds. He saw skeletons, feet, feathers, and many, many white skulls, all motionless. It had been a while since anyone had cleaned the tank or anything had disturbed it.

Brad laughed to himself, remembering another pal named Rusty, who said a water tank was a good place to dunk a deer or antelope to clean it off and cool it after a fellow had dragged it a ways. At the time, Brad had pictured the green junk that collected in some tanks, and now as he saw the accumulated remains of dead birds, he had even more doubts about Rusty's method.

Backing away from the tank, Brad looked again at the corrugated metal, the rugged fence, the standing windmill with the bullet holes in the tail, and the old mill lying face down in the grass. He didn't remember any of these details, or the dead birds, from the year before. He had been intent on getting the antelope off a ways, so that he could clean it and not leave any offal to interfere with cattle that might want to drink. Now, without the urgency of meat on the ground, it was worth a few minutes' leisure to see how time had gone on when most of the world was not looking.

He hunted through the morning, seeing antelope twice but not getting close enough for a shot. He ate his oatmeal cookies at nine, as he had planned, and drove further south until the rolling grassland gave way to broken country. He was tired of driving and lurching and hanging on to the steering wheel, so he got out and walked. He thought his chances of finding antelope down in the washes were slim, but he was glad to get away from the vehicle and stretch his legs.

He was right about not seeing any antelope. He walked the broken country in the full, broad light of day and saw nothing, not even a jackrabbit. As he walked, the thin breeze brushed his face and the song came back to his mind.

> She used to call me darlin'
> Now she don't call me any more.

It played for a while, went away, and came around again.

By noon he was back at the pickup, where he ate his lunch as planned. Then he took a nap, which he hadn't planned. He woke up sweating, with the sun streaming in through the windshield. Climbing out of the cab, he took a moment to clear his head before he stepped onto the ground. He wouldn't call it dizziness, but sometimes of late he had to take a moment like that. When he was sure of himself, he walked around to the back of the pickup, opened the flap of the camper, pulled out a gallon jug of water, and washed his face. The water was still cool, and it felt good.

He took his time getting back into motion. It was two o'clock, and things usually started picking up at around three or four. He drove west until he came to another stretch of broken country, and thinking he could kill an hour or so, he got out and walked again. Things did pick up as the afternoon wore on. Toward the end of his walk he saw two antelope, half a mile away on the slope of a draw, but by the time he moved closer, they had disappeared.

Back in the pickup he was feeling hungry again, so he ate a granola bar from his day pack. That was the way the doctor recommended it—eat a little bit, several times during the day, rather than dump in big loads of sugar. Get plenty of exercise, avoid fat. Brad munched on the granola. Antelope was as lean as a fellow could get and still eat meat.

He drove back to the north, again following the roads that would lead from one windmill to the next. There really was no way of predicting where the antelope might be, but if a fellow moved around in the likely places, he might cross paths with a few. The year before, he had come around full circle and found an antelope close to where he had started out.

Now off to the west he saw a band of half a dozen antelope, strung out and trotting over a rise. He followed them and lost them, but it brought him to a ridge overlooking a broad, open area that sloped up to a row of buttes farther west. Looking at the sky and then at his watch, he decided he would come out at the end of the hunt too soon if he just kept driving and didn't see anything. Starting the circle again seemed like a weary prospect, so he decided to poke around out here, where he had seen more antelope anyway.

Now on foot, he followed a draw to the south, thinking he would stay along the edge of the little basin rather than walk out into it in plain view. The draw led into another one, which angled west, and soon enough he saw the open area again. He followed the edge of the basin, heading generally south. The sun was still warm, but he could see the shadows creeping out from the buttes, and he knew things would cool down at dusk.

Each time he came around a bend, he looked up to his left to see if any animals were grazing in the calm of the late afternoon. It seemed like a good place for antelope—but of course the whole ranch did, and good grass did not guarantee a herd of antelope.

After he had walked for about half an hour, something turned up. A draw was just coming into view on his left when a lone buck antelope came trotting across in front of him at about seventy-five yards away. Out of habit, Brad dropped to one knee to make himself smaller, and as he did so he brought up the rifle. He found the buck in the scope and followed it until the animal stopped and turned. Brad flicked the safety and fired.

The animal disappeared from the scope. Brad thought it had flinched, but he wasn't sure. As he lowered the rifle he could see that the antelope was not lying in the grass. It must have bolted over the rise of ground ahead.

Brad stood up and held still for a moment. It was always good to stop and think after firing a shot, especially when things happened all in an instant. If he had missed, the animal would be long gone, streaking to the south. If he had hit it, it would be lying dead on the other side of the rise, or it would be hunching along up ahead somewhere.

Brad looked to the west, to keep his bearings. The buttes ran generally north and south, curving inward to the east a few miles south of where he now stood. He turned around and fixed on a spot where he imagined he had left the pickup.

Then he turned back to the south and began to follow the antelope.

When he got to the rise where the animal had gone over, he saw it about a hundred and fifty yards ahead. Its white rump was moving up and down as it walked along. Brad was sure he had hit it, and now he knew he had to follow through and walk it down if he could.

An animal that was leg-shot would be farther away, he thought. An antelope could travel fast and far on three legs. But a gut-shot animal would hobble along and stop to rest. If this one stopped, Brad might be able to get closer and bring it down.

After a quarter of a mile, the antelope knelt to rest. Brad was sure it was gut-shot now. He closed in another fifty yards and paused, wondering how close he might get. It was hard to make a clean shot on an animal that was crouched with its rear end toward the hunter. This one had its head turned around to the left, so that the eyes, forehead, and horns formed a dark bead. If it would rise and give a half-turn, or not kneel the next time it stopped, Brad would have a better chance. He moved forward, and the antelope pushed itself up and walked straight away.

And so went the pattern—stalking, pausing, and moving on. Brad didn't want to take a bad shot, because one bad shot could lead to another, and he would run out of shells too far from the pickup and too late in the day. The animal had moved into the center of the little valley and was heading south, with shorter distances between rests. As the pattern continued, Brad decided that each time the animal stopped, he would try moving up to the right, where he could get a broader shot and not have the evening sun in his scope. Twice he took shots that way—and missed—but he was gaining ground. Finally, as the sun was slipping behind the buttes and casting the whole valley in shadow, Brad got a steady shot and ended that part of the hunt.

He looked around. He knew the pickup was at least a mile and a half behind him, and he knew that the easiest way to clean this animal would be to hoist it on the hunter's helper when he had water close at hand. That meant he would have to go for the pickup, then drive back and find the antelope in the dark. He looked to the south and saw a ranch light in the distance, where the buttes curved to the east. He lined himself up with the carcass and the light, got his bearings with the buttes, and started walking back to the vehicle.

Dusk was closing in as the scarlet sunset paled to orange. He remembered a time, a few years back, when he had killed a whitetail doe. It had been late November, with a blanket of snow turning orange in the fading sunset. After field-dressing the deer on the ground he had washed his hands in the snow, then dragged the carcass with his tow-rope, past the spots where the sprinkles of blood had etched the snow. He had kept a steady pace, staying warm but not fagging out.

He remembered another evening, warmer, when he had killed a mule deer at the edge of an alfalfa circle. That one he had hung on the hunter's helper. The image came back to him now, a vermillion sky in the background as the blacktail buck hung upside-down on the gambrel, everything peaceful as the warmth of the carcass went out into the cool evening air.

Sometimes it seemed as if it all came down to heat loss—trying to prevent the loss or trying to promote it.

It was almost dark now. He could still see the ranch light over his shoulder to the south, and he knew the pickup should be somewhere up on the right. After a short, steady climb he made it to the top. Off to his right a couple of hundred yards sat the pickup, its windshield and grille reflecting the last faint grey of twilight.

The cab was warm, and the engine started right up. Brad switched on the lights and put the vehicle into motion. He found the bottom of the basin and turned left. Remembering how he had lined up the yard light with the dead antelope and the contour of the valley, he drove at a steady speed for nearly a mile and then slowed to a crawl. Finally the drab shape came into view in the beam of the headlights.

In the cool of night he set up the hoist and hung the antelope by its hind legs. Then he cleaned the animal, first skinning it and then eviscerating it, working more by touch than by sight. He could tell by the feel, as well as by the smell, that his first shot had clipped the stomach. The cavity was full of rank, bloody mush that he needed to clean out as well as he could. After the initial rough part, he washed his hands, got out a flashlight, and tended to the details.

The moon was rising by the time he had the animal cleaned. He let it hang a few minutes longer as he filled out the tag, detached the landowner coupon, and tied the carcass coupon to the hind shank. Then he slipped a game bag up and over the carcass, hefted the pale form off the gambrel, and swung it into the back of the pickup. As he stowed the hoist and frame, he realized he was tired.

He paused for a moment after closing the tailgate and camper. The moonlight brought back a sense of his surroundings, and he felt his place out on the rangeland, between the buttes and the rolling pastures, far from noise and turmoil. He knew these were good moments, even if life itself seemed a bit spare sometimes.

Back in the pickup, moving north again with the lights on, he felt hungry. He thought of how he would value this antelope meat, parceled out in small packages through the months of the coming year. He hoped he would get a deer, too, but this much was good. Some people despised wild meat in general and antelope in particular, but he knew he would appreciate it for as long as he could eat it. A rancher whose land he had hunted on a few times had told him his wife was diabetic and couldn't eat deer or antelope meat because of the uric acid. Brad looked up uric acid and imagined it must have been hers and not the animals', but he wasn't sure. Either way, he wondered if the doctors would take the venison away from him some day.

It was dark, even in the moonlight, now that he was in the pickup and driving. He had to pay attention to the roads and think about where they were leading. He was taking what he hoped was the most direct way back to the ranch house.

It felt good to be hungry and tired, even if the hunger put him a little on edge. He knew he should appreciate being able to hunt—not only because there might come a day when not just anyone could get permission, but also because there might come a time when he wasn't up to it. He had a lot of hunting behind him, really, and he was glad to be able to hunt while he still had strength in his arms and legs.

The ranch was dark, with no yard light and no lights shining in the house. Maybe the old man had gone to bed early. Brad decided not to bother him at the moment. He would just drive through. He could send the coupon in the mail, with a note of thanks.

About the Author

John D. Nesbitt lives in the plains country of Wyoming, where he teaches English and Spanish at Eastern Wyoming College. His articles, reviews, fiction, and poetry have appeared in numerous magazines and anthologies. He has had more than thirty books published, including short story collections, contemporary novels, and traditional westerns, as well as textbooks for his courses. John has won many awards for his work, including two awards from the Wyoming State Historical Society (for fiction), two awards from Wyoming Writers for encouragement of other writers and service to the organization, two Wyoming Arts Council literary fellowships (one for fiction, one for non- fiction), a Will Rogers Medallion Award for *Dark Prairie* (a frontier mystery) and another for *Thorns on the Rose* (a poetry collection), a Western Writers of America Spur finalist award for his novel *Raven Springs*, and the Spur award itself for his short story "At the End of the Orchard" and for his novels *Trouble at the Redstone* and *Stranger in Thunder Basin.* His recent work includes *Poacher's Moon,* a contemporary novel; *Blue Horse Mesa*, a collection of western stories; and *Field Work*, a retro-noir fiction collection.. Visit his website at www.johndnesbitt.com

"NESBITT IS A TRUE ARTIST."
–WESTERN AMERICAN LITERATURE
A JIMMY GIBBS NOVEL
RED WIND CROSSING
John D. Nesbitt
Published by SpeakingVolumes

"NESBITT IS A
TRUE ARTIST."
—WESTERN
AMERICAN
LITERATURE
John D. Nesbitt
TWO NOVELLAS
Published by SpeakingVolumes

Visit us at www.speakingvolumes.us

A COLLECTION OF WESTERN STORIES
John D. Nesbitt
BLUE HORSE
MESA
"NESBITT IS A TRUE ARTIST."
—WESTERN AMERICAN LITERATURE
Published by SpeakingVolumes

John D. Nesbitt
POACHER'S
MOON
"NESBITT IS A TRUE ARTIST."
—WESTERN AMERICAN LITERATURE
Published by SpeakingVolumes

Visit us at www.speakingvolumes.us

John D. Nesbitt
LONESOME
RANGE
"NESBITT IS A TRUE ARTIST."
—WESTERN AMERICAN LITERATURE
Published by SpeakingVolumes

"For the Norden Boys rings as true as a triangle around the chuckwagon at suppertime."
—True West
FOR THE NORDEN BOYS
JOHN D. NESBITT
Published by SpeakingVolumes

FOR MORE EXCITING BOOKS, E-BOOKS, AUDIOBOOKS AND MORE
visit us at
www.speakingvolumes.us

www.ingramcontent.com/pod-product-compliance
Lightning Source LLC
LaVergne TN
LVHW091040080826
845145LV00002B/568

* 9 7 8 1 6 2 8 1 5 4 7 7 1 *